TESTIMONY OF A
SHIFTER

EMMA PÉREZ

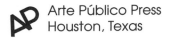
Arte Público Press
Houston, Texas

Testimony of a Shifter is funded in part by the National Endowment for the Arts and the Texas Commission on the Arts. We are thankful for their support.

Recovering the past, creating the future

Arte Público Press
University of Houston
4902 Gulf Fwy, Bldg 19, Rm 100
Houston, Texas 77204-2004

Cover design by Mora Designs
Cover art by Adela C. Licona, Touching Terrains

Working from shared perspectives on the body and its relationship to the natural world, scholar-activist-photographer, Adela C. Licona, photographs scholar-dancer, Cara Hagan, in the dried alkali lakebed of Summer Lake, OR. "Touching Terrains" is an image from the "Shedding Skin" series of photographs that use the lakebed context to explore environmental desiccation and human/terrestrial relations. Assuming there is always more to see, this collaboration searches for ways of experiencing the world through a visual expression of relational inseparability. "Shedding Skin" is a visual production of and for developed intimacies with the land undertaken to cultivate conditions and possibilities for rekindled kinships and sustainable cohabitations with the human and non-human world as these shifts and are reshaped.

23 24 25   4 3 2 1

Para Luzia, *m'ija preciosa,*

Y para mis sobrinos y sobrinas,
Miguel, Elyse, Teodoro, Almita y Azul,

always hope.

CONTENTS

ACKNOWLEDGEMENTS

My story, which came to me in a nightmare on the night of the presidential election in 1980, demanded a genre in which I'm not well-versed. Without the works of Octavia Butler, Ursula K. Le Guin and Ted Chiang, as well as the new generation of Brown, Indigneous and Black speculative writers, I'm not sure I would have had the audacity to write this little novel. I carried around twenty-five pages of a rough draft for decades until one morning in March 2020 as COVID-19 transpired, my academic boo, Juana María Rodríguez, and I agreed to complete our books during the global pandemic. Each morning, we'd text, write and talk until we had manuscripts in hand. Juana María read many iterations and proposed suggestions that lead to improved drafts. I'm so grateful to you for your invaluable encouragement, boo. Later, writer Achy Obejas joined our morning sessions adding her special talents and friendship.

My family and friends are consistent, trustworthy readers. As usual, Alicia Gaspar de Alba listened intently and discussed details with me. I appreciate how we've been writing buddies for decades. My sisters, Yolanda, Cris and Sonja read drafts and probed in ways that helped me clarify and expand the story. My brother, Joe Robert, I thank because he's a kind soul. Without my editor, Nicolás Kanellos, who patiently offered advice and pointed out anachronisms, the novel wouldn't read as well. His questions and precise editing strengthened the novel. I'm also grateful to Gabriela Ventura Baeza, Marina Tristán and other staff at Arte Público Press—all of whom are exceptional and thoughtful.

Friends who listened, inspired or read early pages are many and I list a few here: Natsu Saito, Ward Churchill, Alma López, Angela Crow, Francisco Galarte, Bernadine Hernández, Joy Castro, Ire'ne Lara Silva, Linda Hogan, Michael Nava, Deena González, Antonia Castañeda, Arturo Madrid, Thomas Kinney, Catrióna Rueda Esquibel, Luz Calvo, Deb Vargas, Michelle Tellez, Reid Gómez, Shelley Streeby, Jamie Lee, Macarena Gómez-Barris, Evy Valencia, Ceci Valenzuela, Isra Dominguez, John Michael Rivera, Vincent Woodward—always, John Marquez, Britta Van Dun, Evangeline Mendoza and fellow *tejanas*, Ramona Houston and Koritha Mitchell, who also value brown-black-Indigenous alliances. The students in my class, "Writing Queer Autohistoria," give me hope as they live their truths. Colleagues and staff in the Southwest Center and in Gender and Women's Studies at the University of Arizona continue to sustain me.

Again, I thank Adela Licona and Cara Hagan for their stunning photograph on the cover. I have to acknowledge the first-rate trainers at the AF gym on Silverbell in Tucson. Ian, Anthony, Deb and especially Ysela, my personal trainer for keeping me sane and strong. I owe special gratitude to my co-parent, Scarlet Bowen, for furthering this ongoing adventure with our remarkable crystal child, Luzia.

There's no one like you, *mi'ja. Te adoro.*

PART 1

"Amputate my freckled Bosom!
Make me bearded like a man!"
—Emily Dickinson

"I have always wanted to be both man and woman . . .
. . . to share valleys and mountains upon my body
the way the earth does in hills and peaks."
—Audre Lorde

FEBRUARY 9, 2058

Let me tell you how my body shifted. Just shifted. As a young boy, I couldn't control it. Even when I thought I'd figured out how I transformed, I hadn't. One second, I was a straight-up boy and without warning, poof—I stared in the mirror and there stood a brown, lanky girl. Me. A girl. But only for a few minutes. Once for a full hour, but as I said, I didn't know how, and soon enough I was a boy again. I thought, okay, it happens when I think certain feelings, and if I wanted to change back I'd focus hard, but nothing. The ashen-faced, stout boy I was had to wait until I was older.

All that changed. What I want you to remember, Yareli, is that you're brave. You're our brave daughter. Like your mother and me, you come from a line of proud Descendants—brown and black soul folx from native nations all over the globe. And don't worry about those who hate us, *mi'ja*. They just fear change. Well, there's more to the hate than that. The Woke Wars happened. The Woke Wars salted wounds with bitter hate, and that's when Descendant shifters were rounded up, put in cages, or left for dead. But we learned how to hide and oftentimes we hid in plain sight. Damn Woke Wars. We didn't start them, but we plan to finish them before they finish us.

On days like today when they take me away from you, they put me in a dark interrogation room with a single bright bulb dangling from the ceiling. The Counselor, who plays judge and jury, stands above me while I sit on a plastic, rickety chair. Shadows on his face amplify his pallid skin. He's a pasty looking man whose sole duty is to persecute me.

I tell him my story. The one he wants to hear. He scrawls notes on an electric pad, pokes my shoulders and upper chest with a digital pen, scrawls more, pokes more and stops. He gawks at me, glaring at my gray eyes.

"You're not very pretty, are you? Alejandra?"

I mumble.

"Answer me," he says.

"No sir. I'm not."

"Not what?"

"Not very pretty."

"For a shifter female, you're very masculine, aren't you?"

He studies the file with my birth name, Benito Espinoza.

"Says here you know secrets, Benito."

With the digital pen, he shuffles through pages and pages of an interactive screen.

"Says you know Grand Library secrets," he goes on. "Reserved for the real Residents. Not for the likes of you."

I twist in the flimsy chair. I'm still sore from the last beating. Finally, he nods at the White Guard standing nearby.

The White Guards are the police division trained to keep an eye on us, meaning they watch us, follow us and lock us up when ordered. It's an intimate relationship that they can't resist. Dressed in a white, thick, padded uniform, the Guard on duty prods me with the wooden stick he uses to beat me on the sly or as a command from the Counselor. The club digs into my side, forcing me to stand, and I stumble as he shoves until I fall and rise again. He digs harder into my body, pushing me to our twenty-by-fifteen-foot steel cage in the basement. There're no windows in the building, and dim lights muddle my vision. He chucks me inside, locks the door and bangs the steel web with the wooden club.

"You and your damn stories," he says. "Shut the fuck up."

He's gawky with brown skin, brown hair, brown eyes. I know his type. He's probably the son of someone like me, but in here, he's an imposter. Betraying his own kind. He swaggers away, hitting the steel cages, cussing under his breath.

Now I can start my story for you, Yareli.

AUGUST 24, 2044

I'd been studying in the Grand Library with old men when I saw a woman carry herself with such daring that I wanted to know her name. On that day, she scoured the Library's halls searching for a gray-eyed man.

Let me be clear. I wasn't an elderly man but I considered myself an elder because I was among the greatest of books with the greatest of men in a building with architecture modeled after the grandest of archives. I sat on a red satin, plump high-back chair at an antique desk in a well-lit corner by a window. At the time, I had only seven books in print, and although two were brief one-hundred-page texts, I'd received fair reviews for my beliefs on metaphysics and things invisible and sensory. Of course, the Grand Library's Foundation valued quantity and length, and Residents who had published over twenty hefty volumes were worshipped. My membership was unusual, but the Foundation had been pressured to recruit Descendants, although it turned out we were nothing but show pieces required to uphold the Library's biased principles. You could say I was an experiment recruited to demonstrate that Descendants could be trained to better ourselves, but in the eyes of the Foundation, we'd never be the elite.

That this woman had been permitted in the room for Residents was unusual but not uncommon. She had petitioned the

Head Resident to be allowed to investigate the Egyptian blue scarab. He at times permitted outsiders to visit when they were hunting for a rare book.

From my peripheral vision I spied upon hair so black the light glinted a purple hue upon long, crimped strands. She wore a yellow cotton dress with floral print. Her dusky brown skin glistened, and the fleshiness of her body hummed as she rifled through bookshelves, tossing aside books that seemed to annoy her. As she approached me, I couldn't help but stare at her wide, magnificent hips fluttering the yellow flowers. She slammed a book on my desk, the reverberations echoed throughout the room's high dome of gold lamé lilies.

"*Pinche libro*," she said.

I wasn't sure why she was swearing but I didn't care. Peering into her ebony eyes woke me so abruptly, I crossed my legs. The excitement of nerve-endings resurfaced after nearly a decade of numb detachment. Fortunately, on this day, I wore my robe. All Residents wore white robes in the grand room and, while the robes were not required, they were one of those traditions we enjoyed.

Tamaya, whose name I didn't know yet, opened the book, pointed to a page, looked down at me and asked, "*¿Qué chingaos quiere decir?*"

Of course, I understood Spanish. Almost everyone understood Spanish, but no one spoke it publicly unless they wanted to be punished or ostracized or told to go back to where they came from, which was usually within a twenty-mile radius. I endured the blue eyes of Residents upon me, and their stare raised the hair on my neck. I gazed up at her hoping she'd stop cursing although I was sure that if I asked, she'd defy me. Obviously, she was the disagreeable type and seemed to be testing me. How would I respond? How could I respond?

"What do you people mean?" she asked rhetorically.

I glanced at the graph, relieved she had reverted to English. On the page of an outdated journal, an outline of racialized classifications from the 1790s ranked people by color and social position. The categories were caste designations from "Español" and "Mestizo" to "Mulato" and "Coyote." Skin tones were classified in a color-coded order, which meant that the closer one was to blanched, sallow, pale ivory, the closer one was to a sanctioned God.

Tamaya wiggled her index finger down the column to "*mulato*" and "*coyote*." "*No somos animales*," she said.

I wasn't about to contradict history's judgment that had also offended me. "I'm aware," I responded.

She smiled. "*¿Tú eres el* Benito Espinoza?*"

"Yes, I am," I answered, puzzled that she knew my name.

"*Soy* Tamaya," she said.

She placed her warm hand on mine. I couldn't move. I was mesmerized by this mortal, who bulldozed into the Grand Library seeking my assistance. If the other Residents hadn't reacted when she slammed the book on my desk, I would've thought I was imagining her. But here she was looming over me. Her skin and mine differed in color and texture. She had bronzed, dark flesh that shimmered next to my gray-brown hue, and when her silky forearms brushed against my bumpy skin, I was embarrassed. But she didn't seem to care. Weaving her fingers inside mine, we clasped hands. I stood up, my nerve endings so stimulated that I had to piss.

"I have to go relieve myself," I confessed.

"I'll go with you."

I led her to the spa room where women were not allowed. Residents had their daily massages in the private quarters that hid the elderly men who used the spa for secret shifting. If you peeked inside the windows of the closed doors, you could see well-known, well-established Residents shifting sexes, becoming female in sex and body with a young male shifter brought in from the outside. It was all illegal.

No one noticed I escorted a woman into one of the steam rooms reserved for an intimate rendezvous. They were wrapped up in their own private parties. As soon as I shut the frosted glass door behind us, she pulled me to her, and at that moment, I realized how much I needed her.

RESIDENTS

Tamaya left as suddenly as she had arrived. After she fled the steam room, I was desperate to see her again. I ran to my locker and changed from my robe into street clothes, a uniform of beige khaki pants, tan leather belt, blue cotton shirt and cashmere, beige blazer with suede patches at the elbows. It was hot outside, but I insisted on wearing my blazer with elbow patches because it was how Residents dressed. Hunched over, I tied the shoestrings of my russet leather wingtips, stood tall and glimpsed in a mirror. I decided I was relatively handsome. My wrinkled forehead and gray temples gave a hint of respectability. I sprinted into the foyer, which led to the exit door of the Grand Library. She wasn't there.

"Dr. Espinoza, Benito." It was the Head Resident, Augustus Marcus.

I faced his pock-marked cheeks, which sparkled from the sun's rays diving through the glass dome that illuminated the foyer. The light shimmered on the granite walls.

"Resident Phillip awaits your assistance in the basement."

Augustus Marcus paused as he lectured gangly, blue-eyed boys, some of whom would become Residents if their parents donated generous sums to the Foundation.

Oh, the Foundation did have principles. You see, the league of Residents believed the myths they constructed about their origins as a "non-race." Their ancestors, the so-called original inhabitants, possessed a sturdy, authoritative nature that boasted superiority. As the Ascendant non-race, they reasoned that brown, black, indigenous soul folx like us were lowly descendants, who could never ascend to their genius. But we named ourselves Descendants long before their condemnations and assumptions. As their God's chosen people, "Ascendant-surveyors," they scrutinized everyone and controlled everything. We didn't agree with their punishing God. We had our own. And, I have to admit, I appreciated that young soul folx retitled the Ascendant-surveyors ASSES, an acronym that rang true.

Reluctantly, I descended the stairs to the basement archive and saw a legion of Residents hovering over a fragment of parchment about two inches in diameter. The yellowed parchment had stains and pincushion holes. Under a microscope, a word or two could be deciphered in a dialect appreciated by these Residents. Unlike them, I didn't care to learn their alphabet. Instead, I studied the Descendant dialects from southern continents. The Residents, on the other hand, didn't appreciate Descendant bands from southern continents and mostly neglected what I viewed as valuable texts housed in the Library. But the parchment with scribbles from a northern European country stockpiled million-dollar grants, while Descendant codices collected dust in open bins where sunlight bleached their hieroglyphs. The Residents' focus on Ancient Briton and Anglo-Saxons who had probably authored this fragment was yet another example of what they treasured.

"A new discovery, Benito."

I wedged through the crowd and peered into the microscope. I observed nothing that thrilled me except a fruit fly on the perimeter of the parchment. I didn't smile or frown and my indifference seemed to bother the elders sputtering among themselves. Resident Phillip, whose ruddy face inflamed into redder splotches, shoved me aside.

As he inspected the magnified scribbles, he addressed me.

"If you'll notice, the lettering here completes a previous document." He looked up at me, and his bottle-thick glasses slid down his nose and beads of sweat dripped on the counter where the microscope was mounted.

"Completes?" I asked.

"Well," he paused, "contributes to the document. I get your meaning. Nothing is ever truly complete. Is it?"

He peered at me over the chunky frame of his bifocals. Phillip was old-fashioned and refused to have corrective eye surgery. He probably thought he looked smarter with bulky glasses hanging on his nose.

The document that had them in a spell was an ancient parchment with a fragment that could be part of another missing mandate or could supplement the ones already engraved on the marble pillars of the Grand Library's entrance:

1. Thou shalt not steal land.
2. Thou shalt honor the Impresario.
3. Thou shalt not become what one is not by birth.
4. Thou shalt honor all Ascendants.

I wasn't impressed with their little discovery and didn't agree with their mandates. I swiveled and walked toward the exit.

"The bags are by the door," he yelled after me and gestured toward a pile of garbage bags reminding me of what I meant to him and our colleagues. Resident Phillip wanted a motive to report me, and I eagerly delivered.

I scurried up the stairs and felt a hand touch my shoulder.

"Benjamin, I apologize for Phillip."

"Why, Cicero? You're not Phillip."

"No, but I was like him . . ." He inhaled, paused, exhaled faintly and murmured as he leaned in, "once."

"You're not like him at all. He's an ass."

Cicero tilted his head, grinned, rested his hand on my shoulder and squeezed it. "I was once like you, too, Benjamin."

He breathed deeply, comforting himself, or maybe he meant to soothe me. Of course, he meant to soothe me. Cicero was deliberate in his every move. I'd observed him closely during my seven years in residence and learned from his relationships with the other Residents. He commanded respect without commanding. With a quiet demeanor, he never shouted or spit in your face, never demanded agreement or deference like the others in the Grand Library. I liked Cicero.

"Benjamin . . ."

"Yes?"

"The young woman. Tamaya . . ."

"You know her?" I asked.

"She has a certain, shall we say, notoriety."

"You don't trust her?"

"Oh, nothing like that. No, no, nothing like that, Benjamin."

"Am I expected to guess?"

"There are rumors."

"Rumors?"

"That place she frequents."

"What place?"

"Your luncheons. With the rabble and the woke."

"What are you talking about, Cicero?"

He smiled and puffed out air gently.

"You're a good colleague, Benjamin."

He turned and sauntered down the stairs into the basement archive to join our colleagues. I often wondered how he tolerated them. But at that moment, what unnerved me was that Cicero had filled me with doubt in our brief exchange about Tamaya.

REBEL CAFÉ

Outside, the heat simmered on the pavement and my skin, drenched in sweat, stuck to my itchy cashmere jacket. I pictured Tamaya waiting in the heat and muck, but she had disappeared. Instead of returning to the Library, I decided to have lunch at a place I went to when I wanted to be alone, which was more often than not and not by choice. The café was small. It was rumored that the Rebels covertly controlled the diner. Elder Residents never dared enter the café, because it was in a squalid branch of the city with "too many Descendant scavengers," according to the Residents. The Ascendant-surveyors, ASSES, who were everywhere and nowhere, never dared step inside the "woke" Rebel cell, although it was also rumored that spies sat among us to enjoy the stews with cumin and garlic. It was no surprise Cicero had heard of the café.

"When the hell is Fidel gonna fix up this damn place? We're busting at the seams," grumbled Francesca, the waitress who had just nipped the flesh of her arm, wedged behind the narrow counter.

She continued to grumble as she nodded and directed me to a seat at the counter near her station. The tables were packed with the customary clientele and two or three outsiders seeking the quirky and lewd atmosphere of the café. Among its infamous repute was that it housed a dungeon down a secret passage from the kitchen. Francesca was not as much a part of the colorful characters as Fidel, the cook, who flaunted Mayan warrior tattoos on his arms and on his chest. Peeking through black, curly hair was the tattoo of a red, plump heart with three swords stabbing the center. The man was an excellent chef, even if an occasional chest hair floated in his inspired stew.

Francesca gestured to a chalkboard. After I browsed the specials, I ordered turtle soup, which was not made of turtles at all but instead an amalgam of artificial substances that only tasted good because of Fidel's spices. She poured a glass of tea that I sipped as I scanned *The Hungry Hawk*, the only news daily available on the street and considered propaganda by most, including me. I perused the front page and when I turned it, my jaw dropped. I skimmed quickly, fearing others might witness my shock. On page two, I saw a photograph of Tamaya at a rally brandishing a sign with the word "Scumbag" in large, bold, black print. The rally had been held the day before outside the Impresario's palace. As Impresario and self-appointed Global Leader, he despised rallies, but he especially hated protests in front of his citadel.

I found myself worried for Tamaya, but selfishly, I looked around the café, wondering if anyone suspected I had just had an amorous rendezvous with the woman in the photograph. Was I in danger? Had the other Residents already seen *The Hungry Hawk*? Had they stared at Tamaya in the library because they recognized her? I gobbled down my food. The soup tasted rancid, and I wondered if Fidel had cooked it. When I searched the kitchen, I didn't see him. I asked Francesca, and she said he had a matter in court today, which seemed ordinary enough.

"A traffic violation?" I asked.

"Something more serious."

I thought she would volunteer more information, but she busied herself gliding up and down the counter filling glasses of tea and taking orders. It was then I regarded a curious-looking red-haired woman sitting at the lunch counter. She too was reading the story about the rally. She looked up at me, held my stare, got up and walked out of the café. I could have sworn she gave me a signal to follow. Since I was impatient to find Tamaya, I dropped three coins beside my plate, signaled to Francesca and darted out the back door. The café had no front door. One could only access the space from the back alley, another reason that kept the Residents or their rank from enjoying the cuisine in the seedy location.

When I stepped outside, I spotted the red-haired woman leaning against a trash receptacle piled high with unrecognizable debris. She waited for me to approach. I hesitated. Once she drew a distance from the debris, I was comfortable enough to walk within reach.

"Good afternoon," I said.

"For you," she replied.

"Excuse me?"

"Let's go."

She gave me one of those self-assured side-glances.

"Now," she insisted.

"Go? I don't even know you."

She didn't answer. Out of nowhere, an electric flying machine sped around the corner, barely squeezing through the alley. It was an eVTOL, electric vertical takeoff and landing vehicle, the kind that had swarmed the streets and skies for less than a decade. They were expensive and proved to be too noisy and unsafe, causing so many airborne catastrophes that most were unwilling to take those flight risks. But the absurdly wealthy still had their private eVTOLs, and I figured that this one belonged to someone with enough money to keep it airborne. The door swung open, and a hairy, tattooed arm grabbed my arm and pulled me in as the red-haired woman shoved me from behind.

FOG

I should have been frightened but I wasn't. I say I wasn't because as soon as the red-haired woman thrust me into the back seat of their electric flying vehicle, something pinched my neck, and then I was out. When I awoke, we were traveling beyond the city and into the night. The stars and moon were gleaming above, a dense fog aligned with the horizon and blocked any sight of what we had left behind. At first, I believed I was looking above at puffy clouds, commonly sheer and transparent. No, this was something I'd never seen before. It was thick and ominous with a gray lining.

From my angle, stretched out in the back seat, I spotted stars shooting past, but I realized we were the ones trekking at a high speed.

The woman from the café sat in the driver's seat and, as she steered the golden craft, she turned around and asked, "Is it all you expected?"

I didn't know what she meant. I must have looked puzzled, my wrinkled brow was my reply. She ignored me and turned back to steering. The person sitting beside her was a man I thought I recognized. It was Fidel, the cook from the café. I wondered how long they had all been planning my abduction.

As if to answer, Fidel pivoted to face me. "Sorry we had no stew today, my friend. I didn't have enough time to prepare it. I put an assistant in charge and his culinary skills are lacking."

He didn't answer what I was thinking, but I had wondered about the stew.

"Where are we going?" I asked him and not the female driver because I had confidence in his credibility. He was, after all, a superb chef. It had nothing to do with male preference for male authority.

"You'll see," the woman answered for Fidel. "In time."

"How long have we been traveling?"

"A long time," she replied. "But not long enough."

"How much longer?"

"Not much longer."

I was getting nowhere with her and decided to ask for her name, hoping that a change of subject would make her more forthcoming.

"Your name?" I asked.

"Not important. You, however, are Dr. Espinoza, the great Doctor of Metaphysical Decoding and Reconstruction," she said.

"Not great," I said.

"Ah. Sour grapes, Dr. Espinoza. Sour grapes. You're still upset about the prize. We could have helped you. Our group could have assured that your name was written on every wall from the eastern continent to the western hemisphere."

"I'm not upset," I mumbled.

I gazed out the window and the sky's tint changed from black to crimson. Crimson clouds swirled with webs of pink twinkling lights.

Fidel's eyes reflected on the window. He seemed sympathetic. Or maybe his reflection looked skewed. Maybe he didn't care either and was equally as sarcastic about my failed endeavors. I'd adapted to the mockery dumped on me for having lost a notable prize to a fellow Resident.

"You judge your colleague as not worthy?" she asked.

"My colleague had nothing to do with it," I said.

"Oh, so he was worthy?"

"As worthy as anyone."

"As worthy as you?"

"Probably not."

"You sound disappointed, Dr. Espinoza. Do the Residents know you're upset with them? With their vote?"

"I have complete confidence in the Residents and their vote for my colleague."

They both smirked at the tone of my voice, and I regretted that I'd been so transparent.

"He's not a doctor," I explained, hoping they'd understand my cynicism.

"Making his prize that much more aggravating, don't you think?" said the woman.

"Or more remarkable," I responded.

"Isn't his grandfather a patron of the Grand Library?" she asked.

"Correct," I said.

She sneered and proceeded to manipulate the console of levers and switches that were too advanced for my comprehension.

PhD, Metaphysical Decoding
and Reconstruction

My doctorate in Metaphysical Decoding and Reconstruction did not mean I was a technician. I was a lover of words and things related to words. I didn't bother with machines despite the word "reconstruction" in the title of my degree. There were those who sometimes called on me to fix the radiators in their apartments, crediting me as they would a specialist. I wasn't, and I expressed so often enough, but the turnover of tenants ushered in new ones who saw the label on my door and figured that "Reconstruction" meant I could restore any non-functioning mechanical contraption.

"I don't know mechanisms," I would assure them. "I only know words and things."

"Words and things," they'd ask. "But what things? And what words?"

"Important words," I'd respond.

They would pause and gaze at me, creasing eyebrows tight.

"Why can't you repair the radiator in my apartment? Isn't that a thing?"

The radiators were decades old and functioned on oil and other high-priced fossil fuels available on the illegal market. Either you froze in winter, or you bartered sexual favors with the building's superintendent. He doled out oil to feed the boiler and light the combustion chamber forcing steam through metal pipes to the apartments of his favored lodgers. Another option was available. And that's why they came to me. Whispers in the hallways alerted newly arrived tenants about a gray-eyed Resident whose doctorate in something or other could persuade the superintendent to route steam into their icy living quarters. I did what I could.

PART 2

"Look like a girl when one is a boy (and vice versa)."
—Michel Foucault

". . . the distinction between sex and gender
turns out to be no distinction at all."
—Judith Butler

EL MUNDO ZURDO

The thick fog dissipated the closer we approached a landing, and as if to materialize from nothing, a land mass appeared. The eVTOL floated above a vast field, and in spite of the deafening screech of the breaks, a sizeable group of Descendants waved at us, leaping forward and laughing. Their skin, from sable richness to cream-colored coffee, glistened in the sunlight.

I stared from the window and heard the shouts, "Welcome to El Mundo Zurdo!" And I must admit, I'd only heard about this world, and like so many others, reasoned it was imaginary. El Mundo Zurdo, the world of lefties, you could say, was the name of the Descendant community to which I was abducted willingly. The name honored a philosopher in an Indigenous region bordering what had been Texas. The philosopher, Gloria Anzaldúa, authored theories celebrated by Descendants and shifters (soul folx) called "jotos/as" in her time, at least fifty years ago.

In El Mundo Zurdo, faces beamed, choirs sang. They weren't like people in the city, whose slouched shoulders and sinking heads marked their pitiful lives dictated by the Impresario's Ascendant-surveyors and White Guards. Each time another oil well leaked billions of gallons of mushy crud onto the beaches of the Gulf, each time more plutonium was discovered in the water table of the Rocky Mountains, the planet suffered.

When oil pipelines crisscrossed the land and polluted the surface waters and aquifers, and when the grass and trees were
scorched from unplanned fires, the gluttonous oligarchy ignored
the pleas to stop despoiling the land and air and water and instead reveled in profits. Environmentalists had forewarned us,
but the ASSES refused to listen. As long as the Descendants
were the clean-up crews, they didn't care. I'd heard stories of
Descendants getting infections from dirty needles and razors
used in surgical procedures on the mortally ill from early twen-
tieth-first-century plagues and a multitude of viruses that lingered in the body, edging them toward slow death. One of the
viruses wiped out entire populations. Many who survived ill-
ness had the money for medical care, but not even wealth could
save many others. Diseases and massacres would probably end
us all . . . in time. In any case, the responsibilities of cleaning up
behind the diseased were left to the Descendants. And it was
said that rather than burying the infected deceased, they were
dumped in trash bins along with any devices pricking their flesh.

But here, no one had that wasted look on their face that said,
"My life is hard, it's shovel-shit in the dead of winter hard." In
this place, children played and adults joked in knitted pairs or
groups.

When we disembarked from the eVTOL, we were bom-
barded with gifts of yellow and violet orchids as well as chocolates, dark, bite-size chocolates that tasted of cinnamon. As I
scanned the mist-covered green mountains and white-foamed
waves breaking onto the shoreline of fine sand, I thought I'd
landed in heaven. When I spotted Tamaya, I was even more convinced I'd landed in a celestial paradise. She didn't meet my eyes
or bother to greet me once the children and adults dispersed. Instead, she strolled toward the beach, along with other women who
could have been her sisters or cousins. I was not allowed to pursue Tamaya because the red-headed driver, whose name I still

didn't know, and Fidel held onto me as they led me into a forest, where cabins were built up in trees with stairs leading up to them.

They settled me into one of the cabins and told me to get some sleep because the next day would be filled with activities that demanded my presence. I wasn't sure what they could possibly want from me but at the time I didn't care because they had brought me to Tamaya. It was early evening. The sun set over ocean waves, and, elated, I was unable to sit still. I took off my jacket and shirt and put on a white T-shirt that was placed on the twin bed.

I walked to the beach and removed my shoes as soon as I was on the sand, and it felt squishy and cool between my toes. I rolled up my pant legs and meandered along the shoreline, playing games with the waves as I would when I was a child and my parents would drive us to the nearest beach, two hours from our home. We would wake in the early morning, dress and sleep while my mother drove. With only a short while to play, my brother and I complained when we had to pack our food and return home at sunset. I picked up a seashell and cleaned off the sand with my fingers.

In the city, beaches were not for play or swimming or any human activity except for the disposable Descendant cleaning crews. The water was filled with mercury and other metals that caused injuries among humans who lived along the shore. What had once been exceedingly expensive beach front property was now left vacant for homeless folx who didn't care if they were poisoned. Most vagrants assumed they would die soon, anyway. One-hundred-pound jellyfish inhabited the waters, and if you had the misfortune to meet up with one of them, as drifters often did when they got so drunk that swimming seemed only natural, you could be sure that the one-hundred-pound monster's sting would put an end to you instantly, as it did to those whose bodies would be found floating under bridges.

MARCO

The warm waves enticed me to strip naked, and I dove into the whitecaps, body surfing until I was exhausted. The moon shone over the water, but I couldn't be sure how time was measured in El Mundo Zurdo. The extraordinary thing is that I wasn't hungry. I must have been body-surfing for five or six hours and only now did fatigue catch up to my ancient bones. I didn't ache from the habitual soreness in my frail hip, and my hands were neither swollen nor tingling from numbness as they were prone to. Wherever I was, I felt hyper-human. As if all the earthly ailments in my aging body had been healed. No arthritic pains assailed me. This had to be Utopia.

My sole exasperation was Tamaya's disappearance. I hadn't seen her again, although I was confident that I would see her on the beach. I focused on the moon's glimmer and thought I had only imagined her. And at the moment of remorse and doubt, I became ravenous. I jumped out of the water and walked along the shore naked, my clothes under my arm. The warm breeze turned to a chill, and I dressed hurriedly and ran toward the dunes in bare feet. It was then I stepped on a shell that punctured the fleshy part of my arch. I fell and hugged my foot as blood gushed out of the gash and onto my lap, soaking my pants. The pain was so excruciating that tears streamed down my cheeks.

I hadn't cried since I was an orphaned kid at one of the many camps where we were held like prisoners and bullies would beat me. I was ashen-skinned, not as dark-skinned as they were, and they thought I believed I was superior to them. I wasn't. One day, three of them cornered me in the bathroom. I had just peed and zipped up my trousers when I turned around and Marco's breath teased my eyelids. His hazel eyes shifted to light brown in the sunlit window. He glared at me and refused to acknowledge who we were to each other when his pack wasn't with him. What he did next didn't surprise me. He stepped away and turned his back. Behind him, two boys stood firmly with a broom they'd grabbed from a corner next to a bucket with a mop. They pushed me so hard that I tripped and knocked my head against the tile floor. I must have bitten my tongue or lip because I tasted blood and swallowed it, choking on the sweet, acidic taste. I rolled my tongue in my mouth, searching for a cut, and I must have been distracted because of the pain from the broom stick that they shoved up my buttocks. It was long ago, and I still remember the throbbing I couldn't bear.

I don't believe they had planned it. I think they spotted the broom in the corner and spontaneously went after me. They were so dissatisfied with their lives, knowing they would become garbage collectors. I suppose they assumed I'd become something else. In their minds, seeing me face down, bloodied and with trousers scrunched to my knees—evened the score. At that moment, I couldn't fathom Marco's betrayal. I might have felt a glimmer of the day I'd get my revenge.

When Marco turned his back, he rubbed out every speck of tenderness we'd shared those nights when we would glide with ease, shifting to girls. We had fun playing with plush breasts and girl parts, waiting to catch our breath and coax our stiff penises to fizzle. We loved each other. At least, I thought we did. I must have passed out because I was still lying on that grimy floor when I looked up at Marco's eyes. He cradled my head in his lap, kissed my forehead and brushed back my hair. I sobbed, my chest heaving. That was the last time I cried.

My tears fell on the injured arch, and as they warmed the cut, it seemed to seal. I wasn't sure what was happening or if I had really lacerated my foot. If not for the blood on my pants, I would have thought I had imagined the gash. I stood up, dusted sand from my pants and wiped my T-shirt with a sticky, bloody hand.

THE TREE HOUSE

I rushed back to the cabin and as if to open a path before me, the moon sparked beads of light that guided me up the stairs. I opened the door and saw Tamaya on my bed. She was as stunning as before in attire that shocked me because she wore items that had been banned by the current Impresario and his government, even though women were acquainted with precisely where they could obtain lacy, feminine garments. While men vehemently disapproved of their wives, daughters and female relations wearing such garments, those same men frequented government-controlled bordellos to observe, they said, the women of ill-repute, who wore, well, they wore things like feminine clothes. Such as "sexy" underwear.

≈≈≈

"You already said that, Papi. I'm old enough to hear this part, I'm thirteen," you say with conviction.

"Why don't you to go check on your Mami, *m'ija*?"

Yareli groans and rises slowly. She walks over to her mother, my wife Tamaya, who sits cross-legged in the far corner of the cage with a cluster of women—all Descendants. From the distance, I can see they are hunched over a rectangular manuscript made of deerskin. One of the women has smuggled in the parchment on which they are outlining outer regions unknown by our captors. The Descendant women color in sapphire rivers and emerald mountain ranges. That mapped land is the future, the women assure us. They say it shows escape routes, safe passages to freedom, but I'm dubious about escaping to freedom. And a future? I'm even more dubious.

"Come on, Alex. Give us the juicy stuff," pleads Aurelio, lying face up with his body strewn across the concrete floor as if he were on a sandy beach. He chews on a piece of thin wood he's scraped from the mesquite tree in the courtyard.

"*Ándale*, get on with it," he says.

Aurelio is one of my most appreciative audience members in this cage. He seems to enjoy my stories almost as much as Yareli, my precious daughter, born here in these dark, cold cages. This is all she's ever known and I'm happy she stays with me despite my rambling. I watch her as she hovers over the map and studies what Tamaya and her comrades reconstruct from memory.

I continue.

~~~

This garish style of lingerie could be bought in the brothels, and I'm convinced that the women who worked there and the women that the men went home to were often one and the same.

I imagined Tamaya was pleased to see me despite my resembling a street vagabond, home from his travels.

"Didn't take you long," she said.

I didn't know what she meant, and I can't say I cared. All I wanted was to hold her close to reassure myself that she hadn't been a mirage in the Grand Library. But I restrained myself and stood still. A sea breeze wafted through the cabin, and I stepped forward, facing her, and shut the door.

"I'm not going anywhere," she said, as if to read my mind.

"Where are we?"

"Somewhere safe."

"Safe? Is anywhere safe?"

"In theory, we're safe."

"Theoretically safe?" I asked.

She sat on the edge of the bed and crossed her legs. I admired her as I felt myself grow restless and strange. Tamaya gazed at my chest, and I approached as she sat skimpily attired upon what was to be my bed. She may have meant to distract me from my questions about where we were and what had happened to my bloody foot on the beach. It worked. But what did I care where we were? Stars, beaches, forests—nothing mattered because Tamaya was with me. Her crooked finger beckoned, and I ambled slowly to the twin bed, sweat pouring from my skin. Together, we dampened the sheets and mattress, then fell to the floor, slipping and sliding on the wood in our dance. Her yowling invited wolves from the woodland, and they howled outside our window, perhaps assuming one of their own needed rescue, or maybe they merely joined our primordial harmony of syncopated cries, coveted in that forest night.

She led me into a cubicle, and showerheads sprayed warm water on our naked bodies. Water poured over my back, refreshing me, and I knelt before her seemingly for what felt like hours. We got out, dried each other off and fell into a deep sleep on the bed with the windows opened wide, high up in this odd tree house. For the first time in years, I didn't dream.

When I awoke, I saw her sleeping on my arm and thought, this is *the* dream, and despite the cliché, I didn't care that I was no longer the intellectual named Benito Espinoza. I had transformed corporally into a female body, and this time I welcomed the transformation, willing myself to sustain it for longer than the usual minutes or hours. I felt stronger. Willful.

As a young boy, I discovered that if I touched my sex organs I shifted willingly, fully aware I would return to my "natural" self. I will not bore you with details of a prepubescent boy taking pleasure by sticking his penis in jelly jars or massaging the organ on a beef slab before it's spiced and rubbed for the oven. No longer having Marco as my playmate, I indulged in these blissful experiments that caused longer shifts and soon enough, bananas and cucumbers became my favorite fruits. I kept the secret from both of my mothers after they adopted me from the camp, but I remained discreet and spurned shifter identity early in life. The stakes were high, and I was not the courageous type, as I'm sure you've reasoned by now. Besides, I'd heard my mothers discuss more than once that they wanted me for bigger and better things, which I interpreted to mean, a Resident in the Grand Library. Life outside the camps meant visiting the Library to research books that my mothers said were vital for my intellectual progress. Once, when we were in the great room, my mother pointed to a desk and said, "That's the kind of desk you need, Benito . . . for your studies." I took her suggestion and became a Resident.

When Tamaya awoke, she kissed my nose, got up from the bed and sashayed to the cubicle bathroom. I folded my knees to my tiny, soft breasts and realized how much I had missed my female body.

I got up to stare into a full-length mirror on the wall and studied a somewhat puny, but muscular, body with pert breasts and bushy pubic hair hiding my genitals. I'd become accustomed to myself as Ben with a wide girth penis, even if a bit shorter than average. All of me was usually visible when I was naked, but this femaleness, with its pleats and crevices, made me curious for the pleasures I'd repressed. Mostly, I'd forgotten the contentment of not having to be one or the other but all together something else. I scrutinized my face and, as usual, the features were the same except that I didn't have the five o'clock shadow of a beard on my lower cheeks and my ashen-gray skin was also gone. Instead, my face was smooth and shone cinnamon brown in the light coming through the narrow skylights on the ceiling. I was beautiful.

After Tamaya vanished behind the bathroom door and I had inspected my corporal self in the mirror, I entered an area that resembled a kitchen. Minimalism was definitely the preferred fashion in the tree-house cabins. Nothing that looked like a stove, refrigerator or coffee pot was anywhere in sight. The only item that led me to believe the room was a kitchen was the breakfast nook in a corner with a bowl of fruit placed in the middle of a glass shelf. Mangoes, papayas and avocados, unavailable on the mainland, were piled high in a ceramic bowl. I looked for drawers that might have kitchen knives or cutlery but found none. I remembered that I carried my trusty Swiss Army knife in my pants, which were strewn on the floor. After retrieving the knife from the blood-stained pocket, I peeled a papaya, cut it into cubes and set them on the shiny glass counter.

Tamaya came out of the bathroom, still as naked as I was. She laughed out loud on seeing me, and I thought she might have been laughing at my female-sexed body.

Abruptly, I gazed down at my naked breasts and thought she was laughing at their miniscule size or perhaps was snickering at my thick pubic hair. But it was my effort to make her breakfast that amused her. She picked up a mango, placed it inside a compartment that appeared as soon as she touched the wall—it resembled a shelf or a cabinet. Within seconds the mango materialized, peeled and neatly sliced on two plates that could have been from the eighteenth century, decorated in baroque blues on white with gold-enamel flowers and filigree. She selected a sliver of mango and popped it in my mouth.

"Any coffee in that cubby-hole?" I asked, peeking inside the peculiar compartment that opened and closed as if of its own will.

She poked another part of the wall and an espresso machine came forth with two espresso cups already filled to the top with brown froth on each one. I knocked them both back, placed the cups back on the machine and more coffee spilled into the cups. I knocked those back too.

"Slow down. Too much and you'll get sick."

"I can handle it."

"Whatever you say."

She drank one cup and disappeared into the bathroom to return in seconds fully dressed in cotton shorts and a linen blouse.

"Get dressed. We have things to do," she said.

I showered swiftly, although the heat of the water on my flesh calmed me so much that I wanted to linger. Tamaya had placed a pair of khaki shorts and a clean, white T-shirt on a wooden bench. The tight, somewhat transparent T-shirt embarrassed me, but when she squinted her left eye and smiled, her approval reassured me.

"I need a bra," I said, pressing my hands over my chest.

"No, you don't. Quit admiring yourself and let's go."

At the Movies

I followed Tamaya down the stairs from the tree house and out to a path where the morning sun shone bright on the pristine waves inviting me to go swimming.

We hiked through a wooded area until we reached a door at a mountainside. She knocked twice and it opened, letting us in to a corridor painted orange on one side and purple on the other. The orange wall diverged into another hallway, and we entered a foyer with more passageways, each ascending into narrow corridors with circular stairs.

Although the path confused me, I followed dutifully behind Tamaya as she opened various doors to show me what I could never have envisioned.

We were still a society guided by phenotype and the lottery of genetics. Skin colors ranged from pale beige to midnight black among Descendants, while color hierarchies were imposed on the mainland. Here, in El Mundo Zurdo, there seemed to be nothing like that. Tamaya led me through the long hallway, opening and closing doors where there were children whose skin tones varied in shades of black and brown. The children under five played in a room full of stuffed bears and lions, while the older children romped on swings and slides. In another room, teenagers sat on puffy couches, punching keys of vibrant computer screens and manipulated pixels into vast worlds with forests, orange skies and flying vehicles.

We wound our way back to the purple foyer and she ushered me through vermilion velvet curtains. Theater seats lined the room and a full-sized white screen at the front of the room towered above us. Tamaya nodded toward a seat in the middle of the theater, and I sat dutifully. It had been a long time since I'd sat in one of those archaic film houses. This one resembled the Mayan in Denver when I was a kid before the Campaign for Conformist Ideology tore theatres down. Places like the Mayan were known for controversial films that roused the woke public into action, but the Campaign for Conformist Ideology closed the spaces at the behest of the Impresario, who feared motion pictures that could potentially fire up soul folx. The Campaign assured that no one would ever attend activist theaters again. Or know of them. But I remembered. Having been a lumpy kid, I preferred afternoon summer days in dark, cool, musty theaters when I wasn't in a community library.

Tamaya sat down beside me and deposited on my lap a bucket of popcorn. The aroma of sweet butter and parmigiano-reggiano on the warm kernels elated me. That is, until the movie started. What we watched was anything but amusing. The footage depicted carnage, massacres of children throughout the world. It documented the many holocausts in thousands of camps: the murder of Descendant families and the abduction of their younger children. I had seen that footage as a kid myself before the Campaign of Conformist Ideology became obsessed with any conflicts or events that could provoke people to wake up in anger, leading to more protests and inciting Woke Wars. In response, they banned the disturbing images with decrees called Erasure laws meant to modify our way of life "for the better," according to the Impresario. History had been expunged or altered to suit the Global Order.

I had barely eaten a few kernels of popcorn, when I set the bucket on the floor, unable to stomach children's hands and heads poking out of mud and rubble. I had a strong stomach but not for this. Never for massacred children. A narrator's voice reported statistics of the butchery that had been authorized by the Impresario. I had suspected violence but not this savagery. Like so many in the Global Order, I carried on with daily tasks, not wanting to get involved. But here it was. And here I was. Incompetent, powerless.

"Can you stop it?" I asked Tamaya.

"No."

"Please?"

"No."

I stood up, but when she frowned at me, I sat back down.

"At least listen if you can't watch, Alejandra."

I straightened my back and stared at the screen again.

Tamaya squeezed my hand.

I watched more carnage, regretting having guzzled enough caffeine to rile an elephant. My heart palpitated. I stank of coffee beans, my stomach ached, and I wanted to throw up but instead felt trapped inside a strange corporal injunction that granted no pardon. Rumblings and waves turned into convulsive torment, and I bent over, held my abdomen and felt the warmth of my breasts, a sensation that soothed me briefly.

I twisted around to see the theater filled with adolescents, not children and not adults, but that in-between age when hormones and curiosity of things unknown remain secret from adults. I squinted, unable to see clearly an older child, probably the leader, wearing khaki shorts and a white T-shirt like all of her young friends. Annoyed, I wondered why Tamaya had given me the uniform of adolescents. They pointed at me, chuckled, stomped their feet in unison and gossiped to each other. I slumped in my seat, ignoring the gang of teens who pointed at me and laughed. The more I disregarded them, the more they ridiculed me.

When the screen exposed a recognizable geographic space, I sat up. Snow-capped mountains and fifteen-foot pine trees were nestled in an emerald forest. My mothers had taken me camping in a site that resembled the one on the screen, but the campsite in the movie was harrowing. Barbed-wire fenced in at least two-hundred enclosures that were eight feet by nine feet in length and width. Inside each of the barbed-wire corrals, children had obviously huddled together in the cold, but the ripped tinfoil blanketing their little bodies had not been enough. From the distance, they looked as young as two and as old as eighteen. I wasn't sure. After the camera scanned thousands of specks, the lens cut closer to the frozen bodies of babies. They were Descendants. Brown and black Descendants from all corners of the world. I recognized the white-skinned too. Those who were born orphaned and poor were also left to die. Golden leaves on aspen trees fluttered and quivered in the wind, like tiny hands in prayer . . . or clapping as if to warn observers of the mass slaughter in those Rocky Mountains. I closed my eyes, placed my head on my knees and covered my ears.

Tamaya, who had disappeared through velvet curtains, returned and handed me an aluminum bottle filled to the brim with water that spilled on my shorts. The coolness shocked me awake. She sat down on my left and touched my lips with a flask. I could smell almond liqueur. It smelled like the liquor the White Guards in the camps would sneak into our sippy cups when they wanted us to fall asleep early. I gagged at the nostalgic aroma and sipped.

"Who is that?" I asked.

"Who?" Tamaya asked.

"Behind us. With those gender-bending kids."

"Careful, some don't like that."

"Don't like what?"

"Being named without their input."

"Sorry, my bad," I said.

"No one says that anymore, Alex. Keep up."

"Sorry," I repeated.

"And stop apologizing for stupid shit."

Tamaya turned around and yelled, "*Amorcito,* tell Alejandra your name."

"Don't call me that."

"*Amorcito,*" Tamaya repeated.

AMÉRICA

She was called América, and I wasn't sure why, but I distrusted her. The day I arrived, I saw her with Tamaya. They stood encircled by a group of women animated in their conversation. While I couldn't hear them, I observed closely for a revelation, a clue about América. The women all looked different from each other, with varied skin tones of caramel and sable and plush, round bodies, others tall and angular. América's flesh was violet ebony and her hair, close to her scalp, was a halo of black curls. On her face, there were prominent birth marks that lined one side of her cheek in a kind of astral map steering toward bulky eyelashes. She was so striking that I couldn't resist gawking, and I'm sure she noticed. In any case, she was not who she said she was, although I deduced she had misled herself and believed she was far more altruistic than not. I admit, I too was fooled, believing Tamaya's trust in América. But my instinct told me otherwise and I couldn't help myself. For me, América was unidentifiable.

~~~

I realize I'm telling you too much, *m'ija*, but you'll see what I mean. This is my opinion, not your mother's. You'll have to decide for yourself.

"Why were you so jealous, Papi?" You stretch out on the floor writing in your journal with a crayon nub the color of indigo.

"I wasn't. I'm not." I respond resolutely and even I am aware I'm too jealous to admit that I'm so possessive. I sabotage myself. You lift both eyebrows and smile, your head dangles over your piece of paper with lines and images.

I continue.

SANCTUARY

That evening I wanted another private night with Tamaya, but she was stubborn about transforming me into a willing Rebel, and I still resisted becoming who or what she wanted me to be. We joined a sizeable congregation in a huge edifice constructed of steel rods and wooden planks shooting to the sky in a triangle with the tip pointed to the heavens. The pyramid ascended in the middle of an orange grove, and the aroma of orange blossoms enraptured everyone in its proximity. It was as if the wafting orange fragrance seduced patrons to submit to the building in which meditation and prayer were practiced. But I, Ben Espinoza, remained heterodox even in a body that expressed gender-bending sex.

～⌐～⌐～

"Cut the crap, Alex," said Aurelio.

Aurelio, my only other patron in this prison, prefers to be called Rusty. He crawls closer, using his knuckled fists to swing his torso. While pulling himself up and straightening his left leg, he adjusts the pant leg on the short stub that was once his right leg. The White Guards confiscated his wheelchair and only provide it when they're in the mood. But this doesn't stop Aurelio, who moves with ease, having cultivated a buff upper body.

"You're such a *pendejo*, Alex, I mean, 'Benito Espinoza,'" he emphasizes my male moniker sarcastically. "Damn, you just can't let that go, huh?"

"Let what go?" I ask him.

He shakes his head and gathers his stringy hair into a pony-tail with a thin rubber band.

"Heterodox, my ass," he says. "I see you praying. Don't pretend."

"Can I go on, Aurelio? I mean, Rusty?"

He nods and leans back against the cage, rattling the chain-links. "I ain't stopping you."

"Can I ask you something?"

"I ain't stopping you."

"How'd you lose your leg?"

"Same way you lost your mind, *pendejo*."

I was puzzled that Tamaya brought me here. I'd kept a plastic straw that I chewed on to settle my nerves—remember I had guzzled three espressos. We entered the blessed silver pyramid, where a striking person with shoulder-length blue hair and thick blue eyebrows greeted us. She wore a blue leather skirt with a skintight rainbow-colored tie-dyed T-shirt that exhibited burly pectoral muscles. In her hands, she cradled a thick stack of thin rice paper sheets that the congregants passed out. The single sheets had instructions or advice on what to do during the up-coming ceremony. I followed Tamaya, who held my hand as she coiled around to verify if it was my hand she tugged behind her.

We walked single file behind more than a hundred wor-shippers. Most were already in a meditative state with arms crossed and hands resting inside sleeves or on opposite elbows. I was inclined to follow protocol, but then again, I remembered who and what I was, which meant I had no intention of playing the believer in anyone's holy temple.

Tamaya wedged though the crowd to the front of the sanctuary, tugging me along. We sat down on benches that resembled pews from the early twenty-first century when multiple types of approved places of worship were plentiful only to be bombed and eradicated by the Impresario and his White Guards. If Descendants worshipped in a building, whether church, synagogue or mosque, the edifice was torn down. I didn't worship any gods or goddesses. I loathed the hypocrisies of the religiously inclined who bowed to the god of greed while revering the idiotic Impresario.

<p style="text-align:center">~~~</p>

Again, I'm getting off topic, *m'ija*. As I age, I get more and more cynical and these memories mark every word, every action, everything. My mind gets jammed and keeps recycling the same thing over and over. All I see, all I remember is more greedy fools running the world. I didn't want to die for nothing.

"That's not true, Papi. None of that is true," you say peeking at me from your journal.

You draw diagrams I don't understand or maybe you sketch random shapes, but the concentric circles are something else. Loops and circles weave together in a mesh that looks three-dimensional. You gained these right brain skills from your mother. I'm a dunce when it comes to mathematics or quantum physics or any of the other sciences she teaches you.

"It's all about gravity, Papi," you say to me each time I consider your equations, which only confuse me more. "There's no such thing as time, Papi," you say with certainty, and I'm obliged to have faith in your formulas. "You see, we're all connected."

You draw lines that intersect, linking more circles that loop in and out of each other. You've created a beautiful, colorful, vast web of intricate intersections, and I can only wonder what it all means to you.

"See how they flow? It's like universal life flowing, Papi, and we're all connected. Time doesn't matter. We stay connected."

That you can say things that sound promising makes me grateful, even if I don't understand.

I continue.

We sat in the front row, and as the pyramid filled with hundreds of Descendants, I studied the mantle in front of us. There were no saints or statues of anyone or anything, just a wooden block, thick and mahogany-stained in a dark reddish tint. In silver lettering was the word, VOLUNTAD. Of course, it didn't mean volunteer, even if that was the intent: to gather up troops to volunteer for the cause that the Rebels dreamed up.

Tamaya remarked at that moment. "It's not what you think."

"What?"

"It's not about volunteering."

"I guess I know that."

"Do you? And do you know it's about the will to be and become what you want?"

"No, not really. Well, maybe."

"Willingness, Ben. It's all about willingness. To become, to change, to transform and transcend. These shifters are celebrating. This is our celebration. And we invited you, Ben.

"Alejandra. My name is Alejandra. Look at me. I'm Alejandra."

"In body only. Right now, you sound like Ben."

The crevices on my forehead fold sternly.

"Come on, Ben. Open up. Be willing. Imagine things you've never dreamed."

"Shifting is still illegal, still criminal, still outlawed," I said.

"And you still sound like Ben," she repeated.

"When does this ritualistic ceremony begin?" I asked.

Tamaya rose from the pew and strode to a pulpit that faced the multitude, then nodded to the blue-haired, muscular Descendant in the back of the room. She promptly pointed a remote gadget at the ceiling and thunderous music erupted with a rhythm known to the congregants, who swayed uniformly as if in a trance. I faced the pews behind me to watch closely and I could discern subtle transformations in bodies while faces remained somewhat the same. Confidently, they transmuted among each other so euphorically that I felt my own ecstasy just watching them. There were neurodivergent activists who trembled and shook dancing to their own rhythms, and I envied how they swung and reeled and rocked self-assuredly. It must have been a good feeling.

The congregants continued in meditative joy, and I found myself swaying with those in my pew while others jumped into the aisles dancing in pairs, threesomes, foursomes and some alone in their bliss. A few wore full-length, multi-colored satin dresses, whether male, female, triple-sexed or triple-gendered. The gendered and sexed transformations happened so swiftly that I thought I was observing computer animations of bodies in skillful transition. I witnessed females with thick black beards transform into silky-skinned faces and emerge like kingpins with bulky biceps punching out of white V-neck T-shirts. The array of ecstatic folx rocked, twirled fast and slow, while others waved their hands in the air, performing an awe-inspiring discordance. Happiness engulfed me because happiness spread inside that pyramid.

And suddenly, everything changed. A piercing bang shattered glass, and devotees threw themselves on the floor beneath the wooden pews. Tamaya pushed me down, and I landed hard, hitting my head against the pew's sharp edge. Red liquid streamed from my forehead into my eyes, and I couldn't see, but I did bear the weight of Tamaya's body covering mine, heavy on my back, holding me down as I struggled to get up. I was sturdier in Alejandra's corporeal form, but even as I wrestled, I couldn't match Tamaya's force.

"Stay down," Tamaya said.

"What was that?" I asked.

"Stay down, Alex," she repeated.

Another blast wrecked the front wall of the building, and only steel pillars remained like lone, defeated sentinels. In the distance, three helicopters hovered, and we heard children's cries and screams coming from the airborne machines. I realized no children had been in the sanctuary with us.

At first sight of the helicopters, congregants scurried through the breach that had been the front wall. A rope ladder hanging from one of the helicopters whipped in the wind as a White Guard climbed up while grasping two toddlers sobbing earsplitting cries.

I ran behind and chased the crowd of parents shrieking and fully aware of what was happening. It seemed the White Guards had found the secret island and they were abducting Descendant children in a hasty expedition. We had been distracted in the sanctuary, and the White Guard had taken the opportunity to blast us with gunfire and injure as many Descendants as they could in one fell swoop.

Bullets shot down on us effortlessly. Did the bearers of the guns have souls? Or a heart? Shifters fell to the ground, bodies bowed and twisted. There was no cover; there were no walls or boulders or buildings to deter the bullets. The murderers disappeared into the dusk, an orange sun having barely set as nightfall loomed.

FIGHTS

"Papi, you found the children, didn't you?"

Before I can answer you, we're startled by a loud clamor in the far corner of another cage, where the White Guards hold their weekly brutal games. This one echoes bloodier, if blood can echo. You put your hands over your ears, and I cover your thin, silky fingers with my coarse ones, hoping to shield you from the inhumanity, knowing I can't. You look up at me, and I see your eyes moisten, your eyelids redden. I want you to return to your journal and diagrams that sustain your imagination, helping you forget where we are. But the screams grow louder, and the White Guards' laughter booms. The laughter can't cover up the thud of punches and kicks against a young man's body.

The young man spits and gasps for breath. They have him in a chokehold, a common practice for the White Guards, who relish brute strength against tattooed adolescents. Chokeholds, like lynching, were outlawed earlier in the century, but like any laws that restrict the White Guards, they don't enforce that which brings them so much pleasure.

We hear more hacking. The Descendant women, including your mother, grow silent and bow heads to summon the holy essence of ancestors. Even Aurelio kneels on one knee, propped against the cage wire in meditative prayer, his chin bobbing as he mumbles supplications for himself as much as for the young man being beaten. He could be next. Anyone of us could be next. The random selection takes place in a split second, and no one can object or resist. No one in this dungeon of steel cages moves or speaks. We hear the young man's breath soften. He barely survives. But that's the point: to test the endurance of the tattooed, brown-eyed Descendants. More thuds and bumps can be heard, more roars of laughter from the Guards.

"Who is it this time, Papi?"

"I don't know. I can't see that far."

I lie to you. I don't want you to envision the cruel amusements inside their corral. That you hear screams from the hand-picked Descendant shifter of the week is enough.

"Close your eyes, *m'ija*," I say.

But you strain to see who's in the cage. You have friends here. Some born here like you, others from outside. You've lost friends to these frequent, deadly games. We've all lost someone, and as the infliction of pain grows closer, my wife and her band of Rebels work faster to locate an escape route.

You rise from the cold floor and march to the far end of our coop, stretching arms up, poking your fingers through the wire to pull yourself up on tiptoes. I decide there's no point in stopping you. You'll only invent worse if you can't see for yourself, but there is no worse. This is how the murders happen. For us to witness. I stand up and go to you, wrap my arms around you and pull you away.

"It's Alonzo, Papi."

"It's not him, *m'ija*."

"It is. It's him."

"You can't be sure, *m'ija*."

"I saw his tattoo. His spider tattoo. On his shoulder. It's him."

I don't argue. My attempts to comfort you are inadequate. I'm inadequate. We collapse on the floor, and I place your journal on your lap. I hand you the indigo crayon nub. You gaze up at me, and with my shirttail, I wipe your cheeks dry. You let me comfort you in these trivial ways. Your friend, Alonzo, is resilient and not easily subdued. With the tough ones like him, the White Guards have explicit plans.

Later, when we're allowed to pace in the square courtyard for light and air, we will see his brown limp body hanging from a lone tree. This is how they taunt us and stifle our dreams, but what they refuse to acknowledge is that we're not easily discouraged. We're accustomed to the brutalities and we refuse to believe their cruelty: our only future.

I return to my story, hoping to distract you.

WOUNDS

Tamaya whistled, and from the corners of the forest emerged adolescents of fourteen and fifteen. A few were older, in their early twenties. It was difficult to decipher their ages beneath the night sky. Shadows were cast on their faces from headlamps on their hard hats to guide them down paths. They came in droves to tend to those who were wounded and cover those who weren't breathing. With the composure of an army of doctors, they nursed patients so adeptly that any grief-stricken emotions they may have had dissipated.

I wondered how they could be so efficient, considering they tended to their parents, aunts, uncles and grandparents. I saw no tears on the faces of these young adolescents who had become mature adults in a Global Order that enforced chaos. I wanted to scream. I was full of "no," resounding in my head and beneath my skin. My eyes refused to look upon the mangled, bleeding bodies that lay before me. But this army of youths wore blank faces. They were emotionless as they carried bodies on canvas stretchers through the darkness and into a large space with twin beds lining the room in rows.

Tamaya shouted more, sending the caregivers into the barn-like room the size of an antiquated football field filled with stretchers and beds and piercing bright lights. I followed her, trying to avert my own tears, but when I rubbed my cheeks, my hand dripped blood. Tamaya stood in the middle of the room with bodies strewn around her on beds beneath machines I'd never seen before. A young woman stopped to face me.

"Let me have a look," she said.

"I'm fine. These others need you," I replied.

She was about sixteen years old but handled herself maturely with a technician's poise. After poking at my wound, she pressed my forehead with a moist cloth and scrubbed away dirt. From out of her front shirt pocket, she drew a miniature instrument that resembled a nail clipper but functioned like a stapler.

"What's your name," I asked.

"Not important," she said.

The sixteen-year-old technician squeezed the flesh on my upper forehead near my hairline and made a fold to staple it. I tried not to scream from the prodding and stapling of tender skin and held my breath until I exhaled quietly.

"That should hold. You won't even have a scar," she said.

"What if I want a scar?"

"One of those, are you?"

The question unnerved me because I didn't accept that I was ordinary, despite insipid grumbling to convince anyone who might listen that I was an average nobody. Humility was its own circuitous route.

"One of who?" I had to ask.

"Oh, you know, the type that's eager to flaunt battle wounds."

"I don't need to flaunt battle wounds."

"Don't you?" She rushed off to tend to those in far more need than my insignificant hairline gash.

～⊃～⊃～⊃

"You're so dramatic, Papi. You barely got hurt."

"It was a lot of blood," I respond.

My melodrama is meant to distract and amuse you, Yareli. These are the moments you roll your eyes and grin with that nearly full-toothed mouth. A prominent front tooth is missing, and you enjoy watching people's faces when you smile at them. You say that you learn the depths of their souls by the way they respond.

"How do you figure that, *m'ija*?" I ask.

"Simple, Papi. The ones who grin back at me are the ones I trust. The ones who look away, I never trust." She looked up at the high ceiling that reached up forty or more feet and then spoke pensively. "Unless they're neurodivergent activists, and then I just trust them because well, I just do."

"Your scientific method is impressive," I respond. "Can I go on?"

You nod.

〜〜〜

The young technician was right. I wanted recognition for having survived the blast while running with devotees after the abducted children. I wanted praise for running toward and not away from the gunfire. I roamed around the zone filled with twin beds holding bodies maimed in ways I can't and don't want to describe. I suppose I was in shock, and the minor cut on my hairline kept me present the way insignificant aches keep us present because of the annoying sting, if nothing else. I searched for Tamaya in the crowd and resigned myself to spending the rest of my years searching for her. Not a pleasant prospect, but here I was and here I would be, and so long as she inhabited the world, I would pursue her.

"Quit daydreaming and help us. Or doesn't the Doctor of Metaphysics and Reconstruction know how to enter this mayhem into computers?" Tamaya shoved some type of electronic pad to my chest, but I stuck my hands in my pockets.

"How did they find us?" I asked. "And it's Doctor of Metaphysical Decoding and Reconstruction."

She lifted her head to look at me and promptly paraded up and down aisles, inspecting the clipboard-sized electronic gadgets held by the technicians. The clipboards, or minipads, ran computerized files about the maimed, their chances of healing and the injuries that would now control their lives. I followed behind her.

"How did the White Guards find us? I thought we were safe."

"Spies."

"Spies?"

"Spies," she repeated.

"I'm not a spy, Tamaya."

"Don't be stupid. This could only be someone who knows how to lift the veil of fog that creates our sanctuaries. Someone helped the White Guards. And that clearly wasn't you."

"What do you mean?"

"It's a practiced consciousness. Descendants of fifth-dimension consciousness transform the fog into a geographic space."

"You're saying this place isn't real?"

"Of course, it's real, Alex."

"But you just said it's an imagined space."

"Real. Imagined. Real. Imagined."

"Huh?"

"It's a never-ending cycle. You must be real to imagine what will become real, and yet without having been imagined, there can be no 'real' real because all that is to become real begins in the imaginary."

"That's incredibly confusing and highly unlikely."

"Didn't your mothers teach you about intensities of consciousness?"

"They taught me a lot of things."

"Were you listening the day they taught you about the dimensions? Even a five-year-old knows this stuff, Alex."

"I listened. The stories were fairy tales for this five-year old."

"So, you do know?"

"Of course, I know. My mothers ingrained me with that *mierda* but it means nothing to me. There's no such thing as dimensional consciousness. They're myths."

"We all inhabit various dimensions, Alejandra."

"How do you know? You can't prove it."

"You're right. I can't prove it. I can't prove to you that I love you either, but you know it because you feel it, don't you?"

I was silent.

"Well, your actions could prove to me you love me."

"What actions? Like bringing you here? To El Mundo Zurdo? Is that what you mean? I bring lots of folx here. Does that I mean I love them too?"

"How should I know?"

"Damn, Alex. You just won't take that leap of faith, will you?"

"Leaps are dangerous. Science is real."

"Look around. We wouldn't have the capacity to heal without science, Alex. You can be so limited, you know that?"

"Alright then. Answer this for me. Do tears have the capacity to heal? Here in this imagined space of an island?" I asked.

"What?"

"The day I arrived, I went body-surfing and cut my foot. When I cried, I saw my tears healed the gash."

"Yeah, that can happen," she said.

"Why can't you heal the wounded now? With tears?"

"Oh, some can be healed if the cuts and abrasions are minor. These are more serious. But you see these technical wonders?"

Tamaya pointed to platforms with mechanized beds. Hovering over each bed were tubular wands on wire cables to extend and maneuver close to patients.

"Made in China," I said after inspecting the small print.

"What used to be China. Their acupuncturists and holistic healers were ahead of the curve. These wands have light waves that activate the body's ions in a kind of thermal effect that mends flesh and restores cells faster than if patients were just lying here in bandages."

"They work?"

She shook her head and focused on the buttons of a thermal wand and adjusted the tip to blow air into a Descendant's shoulder that had been shattered by a bullet.

"What do you think," Tamaya said.

I studied as she manipulated the wand an inch from the gaping hole that exposed bone drenched in blood. The blood evaporated from the heat source, licking up the puddle of liquid.

"And América?" I asked.

"Why do you ask?"

"Aren't you worried? Have you seen her?"

"América is resilient. More than either of us."

"But have you seen her?"

Tamaya squinted, staring into me. I must have been transparent.

"Don't worry. No one will suspect you're the spy. Your consciousness is much too shallow," she said.

And with that poignant statement, she hurried off to more teen technicians, who held the clipboard-like mini pads that scrolled computerized data.

As I watched Tamaya, I assembled notes on the electronic pad she gave me, recording what I witnessed in that vast triage. When América materialized from the orderly chaos, she roamed the narrow aisles. I monitored her movements, aware she'd find Tamaya and, within seconds, América stood next to her, confiding in such an intimate manner that I became unhinged with jealousy. Their faces touched intimately, and I thought I witnessed kisses resembling light pecks on each other's cheeks.

They spoke, and I couldn't read their lips from such a distance. América brushed back a hair strand from Tamaya's eyes, and they each smiled. When América peered closely at Tamaya's clipboard, she frowned and wagged her finger in Tamaya's face, hissing until spit sprayed from her mouth. Tamaya punched into the clipboard faster. I couldn't hear América, whose irate deportment intensified as Tamaya's disregard deepened and persisted with a composure that enraged América. Unexpectedly, América slapped Tamaya's face, pummeling her so fiercely that she fell backwards and landed on her buttocks. With her hand over a bloody nose, she rose to her feet and smeared blood across América's face, who promptly rubbed it off with the hem of her blouse and stormed out of the building.

I couldn't resist. I chased América, trailing behind quickly, fearing I might lose her through the dim path lined with pine trees. When she paused to stand on the crest of a sand dune, I hesitated, aware she could see me if she turned around. As she stripped off her blouse and pants in the moonlight, I thought she sensed my presence. The outline of her fine, rounded body shimmered. She pressed her hands over ample buttocks, caressing each cheek with a fastidiousness that convinced me she was aware I was nearby. Naked, she ran into the white crested waves, and I lost sight of her when she dipped below. I wanted to run and dive down to find her, but I hesitated again when a memory of another place unnerved me because I'd buried that memory. I circled back and headed to the treehouse, fully anticipating I'd see América again, even though I cringed at the thought of who she had been. I wanted to be wrong.

THE RETURN

The following day, Tamaya woke me up at daybreak.

"It's time," she said.

"Time?"

"Time to go."

"Go? Where?"

"Dress quickly. You don't have much time."

My slacks and shirt were laying at the foot of my bed, washed and ironed with such precision that the starched crease on the trousers felt rough against my skin.

"Thanks for the starch," I said.

I felt strange in Ben's clothes again, which fit loosely around my waist. I bent over to roll up the pant legs and tightened my belt. Tamaya ignored my comment and furrowed her brow as she punched words and numbers into her electronic clipboard. I wasn't ready to leave.

"I want to help find them," I said.

"You don't know what you're asking, Alex."

She didn't look up as she typed data.

"I said I want to help."

Tamaya fixed on the screen that popped up messages in amber and blue hues.

"Please. Let me do something to help find them."

"Suddenly you want to be a hero?"

"I didn't say that."

"No, but you inferred."

"Oh, I get it."

She still wouldn't face me.

"You don't trust me, Tamaya."

"Trust you?" Tamaya mumbled into her screen, as if to find a response inside the display.

"That's it, isn't it? You don't trust me."

She shook her head and tossed the mini pad on the bed. "No, you don't get it, Alex. You never have, and I doubt that you ever will get it. Even now."

"Even now? What's that supposed to mean?"

"I have to spell that out for you. too?"

Tamaya glared at me and held her breath. I matched her glare as we stood quietly facing each other.

"You'll miss your ride if you don't hurry." She squinted.

"I don't care if I miss it."

"Go, leave."

"I said I'm not leaving. Not until I know more about the abducted children."

"What do you suppose you're going to find out?" she spoke firmly and slowly. Her face flushed.

"I don't know. Something, anything," I blurted. "I don't want to leave until I know something."

"Right. Okay. Here's something for you to know, Dr. Espinoza. While you play in book stacks with your colleagues, these abductions happen every day. Yes, that's right. Daily. And where are you? You don't seem to care then, do you? Ben?"

She spoke coolly, but I cringed because she said my other name like an accusation.

"You have nothing to say?" she asked.

She was right. I had nothing to say.

At precisely 5:55 a.m., the electric vertical take-off and landing aircraft soared, disappearing through dense fog. I had assumed the vapor was an anomaly, an unusual blanket that clotted the sky, but now, I witnessed the phenomenon that Tamaya had explained. That the fog was an illusory thing controlled by Descendants with higher consciousness, I was still doubtful. . . .

When the vehicle finally descended through the haze, I scrutinized a sea of whiteness with creases of blue and black sprinkled throughout the miles of terrain. Upon closer approach, a gray asphalt parking lot materialized, and that's when I saw thousands of white elastic gloves cluttered across the lot with the occasional blue or black gloves enhancing the whiteness. The virus had returned, infiltrating our public lives, compelling us to stay safely in the private cubicles that were our apartments and small houses. Unless you belonged to the Impresario's exclusive league who lived in mansions with bunkers filled with much more than they needed to survive, you were still at risk.

I looked at the driver, speculating if she also had spotted the grim emblem from the past that revisited the present. She nodded.

"We were expecting this," she said.

"I know," I said.

We were both quiet.

"I wonder how many will die this time?" I asked.

"As many as they want. It's always planned."

"Have you been immunized?" I asked.

"Yeah. I had to fight to get the vaccine, but I don't have to tell you that."

"No. You don't."

"Being a Resident has privileges, doesn't it, Dr. Espinoza?"

I couldn't answer. I wouldn't answer. I'd been guilty of taking the vaccine boosters each time the virus exploded again in its latest, sturdier strain. It was population control on a broad scale. A way of leveling Descendant shifters without taking responsibility for executing them. You might as well have lined us all up in front of a nineteenth-century firing squad and riddled bullets through our flesh, because that was how the virus infected us. The infection took everyone and anyone, but the poor were most effected, and the parking lot below proved my point. As usual, brown and black Descendants were the cleanup crew wading through the germ-infested parking lots to gather germ-infested gloves tossed to the ground by the more privileged, who didn't care who would be infected. At least I wasn't in that class of inhumanity. Instead, I belonged to the sort buried inside the Grand Library with the luxury of avoiding the virus like an implanted bomb. Would it go off? Or would it lay dormant until it attached itself to another host, perhaps exploding in that one? It was as if we were all walking time bombs without knowing which ones had been activated. This was the new Global Order. How do you make revolution against hidden, unpredictable viruses that keep evolving?

After we passed the cloudy vapor, I no longer inhabited Alejandra's body, although my thought processes seemed more like hers. My mind and body were not at odds but instead acquainting themselves while my heart's desire became more palpable, but for what I wasn't sure. I loosened my belt and pulled down the rolls on my pants to lengthen them again. My body was Ben's, and I believed I had no control.

We landed on the identical spot from which we had departed. The driver didn't speak much for the duration of our trip, despite my attempts to cull information from her. As soon as the aircraft landed, I was dispirited.

"Don't worry. If you had the vaccine last time, they say you'll be fine for this round."

To be honest, I wasn't considering the virus. The driver turned around to peer at me.

"That steel briefcase. On the floor beside you."

"Yes?" I asked.

"Take it with you."

"What?" Confused, I shook my wrist and jangled the chain tied around it. "When?" I asked.

"Oh, you fell asleep," she responded. "Don't you remember?"

"For a second, I might have dozed off."

"Just take it with you," she repeated.

"Why?"

"Just take it."

"And you're not going to tell me why."

"You'll know. Soon enough."

I climbed out of the vehicle. The red-headed driver shifted into high speed and soared into the sky and through the smoky fog blanket drifting up there somewhere. The journey had taken most of the day, and the turbulent ride, along with the weeks' events, had exhausted me. I was aware of two vital details: I had shifted back to Ben's body and a briefcase was clamped to my left wrist with a chain. An albatross clinging. She had managed to fasten the thing to me while I was asleep for what felt like seconds. Time moved slower or appeared to move slower. I was becoming more aware of time and its paradoxes as well as the way we as a human species attempted to tame the untamable. We made time an entity to yearn for when we feared we were running out of it. And with this gray steel briefcase wrenched around my wrist, time trapped my every step.

In the alley near the café, I ruminated about my predicament until I decided to enter through the customary back door and was immediately contented to see an old friend.

"Fidel! *Amigo*!" I yelled but perhaps too stridently.

On seeing me, Fidel pushed his index finger against his lips and pointed to an empty seat at the lunch counter. Dutifully, I sat down and noticed that all occupants in the café were staring transfixed at the news screen, which provided our daily dose of propaganda. A sprinkling wore face masks to deter the spread of the virus, but most didn't wear them anymore, either out of defiance, sheer stupidity, or just faith in their vaccinations. I belonged to the latter.

I hadn't missed sickening untruths from the Impresario, a man whose mendacity matched his lazy demeanor. His hair had hints of orange, a color that also tinged his flesh, which seemed covered in scaly scabs. Many agreed that too many tanning cubicles had done irreparable damage to his skin and that each day he smeared a tint all over his incrusted flesh to hide the scabs. Others said he had been born of the Descendants and, to infiltrate the ranks of power, he had tarnished his flesh with chemicals to burn away the dark brown skin.

He wouldn't be the first person to attempt skin-lightening to escape bigotry. In fact, suspicions flourished in the Grand Library about many members who had similarly burned away bronze flesh. Surgery also allowed them to transplant brown eyes for the favored blue. These were costly, painstaking surgeries, but the Impresario and his cohorts had pilfered enough wealth to have that surgery and numerous others. We all knew that. It was easy. All the affluent had to do was pick up a vagabond, promise them food and alcohol for the rest of their lives and they willingly had the procedure that plucked out their blue eyes, leaving empty sockets in their heads forever bandaged to hide the cavities. The excavated brown eyes were destroyed, and the drifters became blind for paltry compensation.

⇜⇝⇜

But I digress.
"What was on the screen?" You ask.
"I didn't ask, Papi."
I inhale deeply and continue.

THE PALACE WALL

It was frightening. Another tragic massacre. I had only been gone a week, and in that time three young Rebels had whimsically adorned the exterior walls of the Impresario's palace with caricatures of him and his family of two old men and an old daughter who wore sunglasses in public.

The videotape from security cameras recorded details of the incident on the screen. One of the adolescents was scaling the palace wall while two others painted a chunky, orange mule with the face of the Impresario. Neither noticed their other friend scale the wall, but the camera unmistakably caught him spraying the barricade in black, bold letters, "WE WILL WIN THE WOKE WARS!!! The boy's hand flittered swiftly and inscribed "W5!" all over the barrier." An excruciatingly shrill alarm sounded off, but he was undeterred from his mission. Startled, the two Rebels sprinted from the scene, then one stopped and motioned to the other, probably realizing their friend was missing. When they scurried back, they saw the missing Rebel leap from behind the seven-foot wall and dash toward them. But it was too late. The Impresario's White Guards advanced swiftly and caught the three Rebels in the customary wire nets that blasted electric shocks at whomever was ensnared. The White Guards sprayed water at the culprits already suffering from the electric jolts. The water, coupled with the charged shocks, electrocuted them so harshly that coming back from unconsciousness was unlikely. They were burned. All three of them. The sight of flesh fried and smoking was unnerving.

After the group of twenty-two White Guards had murdered the two boys and a girl with impunity, it was later determined that they had been fifteen and sixteen years old. The Descendants were angry, so angry that the following day, hundreds of Descendants stormed the White Guards, who wore bullet-proof vests and thick impenetrable suits of rubber. Plastic shields protected every inch of their faces. They brandished heavy weapons and shot fireballs that exploded into hundreds of charged pellets emitting gaseous poison. Some of the fire pellets combusted and others burrowed into flesh slowly killing the victims. Twenty-two guards annihilated two hundred or more Descendant protesters, who were no match for the high-tech weapons and attire of the White Guards. Another massacre ensued. Another spontaneous rebellion was quashed. The details weren't hidden.

I couldn't move from the sight of the mangled bodies piled on top of each other, bloody and bruised. It was almost as if the smell had invaded the café. Impulsively, I bent over, folded my unchained arm across my stomach and held my breath to keep from retching.

"You had to do something, Papi."
"I know."
But I was at a loss then as I am now in these cages.

When the news screen displayed the carnage of limp, blood-soaked bodies strewn in front of the palace wall, silence overcame the café. I gazed down at my hands resting on the counter, my left wrist chained to a conspicuous object that I still had no idea what to do with.

"What's the matter with you, lazy asses?" A girl screamed.

Her skin was stunningly dark, burnished copper, and she looked about thirteen years old. Maybe older. She certainly acted as if she was older. She howled at the screen until she turned to stare at the seated clients. Her gaze landed on me. I was dumbfounded. I had no retort to the comment about "lazy asses."

"Look at you. You're all a bunch of pitiful, useless, lazy asses," she groaned. "They were my friends. Those boys and that girl. Murdered. For painting a stupid wall." She wiped her nose on a frayed, beige cotton sleeve and slumped back down, hanging her head over the wooden table. Her shoulders heaved.

I wanted to approach her, not knowing why or what I could possibly say to a girl whose best friends had been taken from her on television. I looked up at Fidel, who read my mind and set two bottles of rare mineral water in front of me. He tipped his head toward the girl. I wrapped my right hand around both bottle necks and clumsily grabbed the gray steel suitcase handle with my left. I was becoming increasingly irritated with my burden. Most clients had returned to conversations with each other, while others read their copies of *The Hungry Hawk*. In other words, it was as if nothing had happened. Tamaya was right. These slaughters had become a daily occurrence, and no one disrupted their habitual routine, with the exception of the Descendant girl who had shouted at us.

I placed the bottles on her table and sat down in a flimsy plastic chair across from her. She didn't look up.

"I brought you some water," I said.

"Huh?"

She finally looked up at me. Her brown eyes, sad and exhausted, had purple circles underneath the paper-like flesh. She was too young to look so tired.

"What do you want, old man?"

"Old man?" I asked.

"Yeah. Old man."

"I'm just offering you water. That's all. And to say I'm sorry. About your friends."

"Yeah. Sure. Thanks, old man."

I winced and got up clutching the steel briefcase's handgrip, a gesture that interested my fellow young citizen.

"What's that?" she asked.

"What?" I glanced at my left hand and held up the briefcase, which was unusually light but still cumbersome. "This?"

"Yeah. What's in it?"

"I don't know."

"Yeah, right. Never mind."

"Seriously, I have no idea what's in here. Someone gave it to me."

"Who?"

"I don't know."

"Fine. Don't answer my questions."

"Okay, kid, here's the thing."

I was hoping she'd talk to me. To be honest, I wasn't well-versed and hadn't been for a long time. That is, ever since I'd joined the Residents at the Grand Library, I'd forgotten the dialect of my neighborhood. Purposefully.

I began hoping I would sooth her grief trying my best to use street vernacular, I heard faint musical chimes. The melody was of the variety that played when ice-cream trucks would trail through neighborhoods and children would run outside screaming at the truck driver to stop. I lingered to relish in the nostalgic tune. My body released palpable sorrow. Those were not innocent times. I was nostalgic for that which had never been, except as an imposition from the present on to the past—a made-up history to appease a contemplative mind that found no rest. We had failed our children.

"No reason to cry. Jeepers. Get a hold of yourself," she said.

I cracked a smile. No one used words like jeepers anymore, and I wondered where she'd heard it.

"Well?" she asked.

"Well?" I replied.

"You were saying, here's the thing. Here's what thing?"

"Nothing. Never mind, kid."

"Fine, old man. But at least tell me what's in the briefcase."

"I don't know."

"You don't know?"

"Someone told me to take it."

"And you listened?"

"I had no choice. The chain was already locked on my wrist."

"Have you tried opening it?"

"Opening it?"

"Yeah. With this button here."

I rested the briefcase on the wobbly table to inspect it further, not sure if I wanted to expose the contents, but she pressed a button and the latch popped up. The brown girl lifted the top of the case and peered inside.

"It's empty," she said.

"What?"

I flipped the case around, looked inside and saw empty rows of violet felt cloth. I frowned, and the girl giggled.

"You really didn't know, did you?" she said.

"No, I didn't. I told you. I may be many things, kid, but I'm not a liar."

"Well, I may be many things, but I'm not a kid."

I snapped the case shut, grabbed it and walked toward the door of the café.

"Wait a minute. I can help you pick that lock."

"What lock?"

"The lock that's keeping you shackled. But hey, maybe you like being in chains."

I was curious enough to walk back to her table to see if she could complete the task that was reserved for menfolk from the last century who broke into bank vaults and were named Jake or Max.

"What's your name, kid?"

"You can call me Lucy."

"That's your name?"

"It's what I said."

"You don't respect your elders, do you?"

"Why should I? I don't see you doing anything to change the shithole we're living in."

Lucy pulled out a hairpin from her tangled mess of brunette tresses and employed the ancient tool with such expertise that the handcuff fettering me clicked and I was as a free man, so to speak.

She beamed wide, exhibiting pride in her proficiency. "There you go."

"I suppose I should thank you."

"Whatever, old man."

"I'm not that old and I have a name."

"Whatever, Dr. Benito Espinoza."

"You've heard of me?"

"Yeah. You're one of those self-important dick Residents at the Grand Library."

Explosives

With that last insult, I marched out of the café. Ever the cynic, ever the outsider, I resented being named as a member of elite or pompous circles. I stomped on the cracked pavement, cursing the girl I'd met and cursing myself for the life I'd chosen as a Resident. But I'd paid my dues in camps. I stormed back into the café.

"Fidel, where's Lucy?"

"Who?"

"Lucy! The girl!"

"Eufemia? She left."

"Eufemia?" I paused. "She lied?"

"Yes, that's what she does. She called herself Eufemia when she started coming here last winter. Looking for shelter. That's street urchins for you."

Fidel was not one to judge the homeless and when he said "street urchins," he wasn't being demeaning. He had a warm spot in his heart for them.

"Where can I find her, Fidel?"

"That, my friend, I do not know."

"Has she ever suggested where she lives? Her home?"

"Street kids have no home. You know that."

"The street kids live somewhere."

"Why the interest, Dr. Espinoza?"

"She was upset. About her friends."

He paused, lifting his goateed chin parallel to the ceiling. "These matters can't be rushed."

"What matters?"

Fidel's eyes scanned the café, which had emptied out except for a couple at a far corner table sitting so close that they must have inhaled the scent of the day's spices on each other's breath. That did not reassure Fidel. He gestured again with his furry chin toward the counter that divided the kitchen from the seated customers. This was my opportunity to speak openly with Fidel about the Rebel stronghold far from where we were, or maybe it wasn't far at all. How could I know?

I strolled into the kitchen, and he snatched the briefcase, unclasped the lock and looked inside. He lifted the velvet cloth and searched beneath, letting his fingers probe each corner of the case.

"There should be two," said Fidel.

He held a disk-shaped object in his palm and carefully returned it to a hidden corner beneath the velvet cloth.

"Two? Of what? What is that thing, Fidel?"

"The path to liberation."

After closing the case, he set it in a drawer beneath the counter and locked it. I could breathe again, no longer responsible for the albatross that had been in my possession.

"Now you do have a reason to find her."

"Lucy?"

"There should be two devices."

"What devices? What are they?"

"I told you, my friend. The path to freedom. And I can assure you, the Rebels will not be pleased with you."

"With me? I didn't steal whatever that thing is."

"You were in charge. And you allowed an adolescent girl to fool you."

He stirred the gigantic pot that emitted the comforting aroma of cilantro.

"Taste this. I need the opinion of a scholar."

He shoved a wooden spoon in my mouth to distract me and avoid any more questions I might have about the devices in the briefcase. My tongue burned from the chili pepper and boiling broth. I coughed and sneezed repeatedly. Fidel smacked my back hard and handed me a glass of cold water. I choked as I drank.

"Fidel, are you trying to kill me?"

"I thought you were an aficionado of spicy *chile.*"

"I like *chile.* Just not so hot," I said.

"There is no other kind."

I shook my head, knowing I couldn't win a debate with a culinary master.

"Fidel, will you do me favor?"

"You are not in a position to ask for favors."

"Will you give this to someone for me?" I pulled an envelope from the inside of my blazer pocket. While on the return trip, I'd scribbled a note that I knew I couldn't deliver.

"I can't take that." He held both palms up to dissuade me.

"But why?"

"*Amigo,* you should be more concerned with the device in Lucy Eufemia's possession."

"I don't even know what it's for."

"Don't you?"

"Are you going to tell me?"

"It's obvious. The tiny explosive will do damage."

"I want nothing to do with that."

"Don't you?"

"I don't."

"You do realize that your journey to El Mundo Zurdo was a gift."

"Oh? And now I'm supposed to do what? Payback time, Fidel? Because I never signed up for explosives and devices like this."

"The minute you stepped on to El Mundo, you signed up, *amigo*."

"Uh. No. I did not."

"The reluctant warrior, Benito. Such a tragedy."

"You're saying I'm tragic? For staying out of this mess you call a revolution?"

"Who said anything about revolution? I'm just following orders and I can tell you that Tamaya is not going to be happy with her reluctant warrior if you don't retrieve the missing explosive."

"How am I supposed to do that, Fidel?"

I was losing patience and preferred to go on with my day without having to answer to Tamaya, who had pushed me off the island. It was as if a puppet master had manipulated my every move and I was jumping erratically like a toy the Rebels maneuvered, pulling strings in directions that suited them. Fidel glared at me and nodded.

"Please go," said Fidel. "I'm preparing for the dinner rush, and this stew will not cook itself."

MARGIE

I held on to the letter and strolled out of the café disheartened. I walked the empty streets cursing my loneliness and stupidity. Slowly, I trudged up the steps to my loft apartment, punched in a keycode, and the door creaked open. My breath evaporated like fog into an icy atmosphere. In one brief week, August summer heat had veered into September's frigid chill. I lingered in front of the long mirror in my bedroom, assessing a spongy body and brushing my rough hands across my flat chest, feeling awkward because I had started to appreciate my female-sexed form, like never before. This man I saw in the mirror was somehow becoming foreign to me. My heart, its desire, had changed. I couldn't articulate what was happening and the mirror only reflected a facade hiding who I really was. The reflection appeared inauthentic, like an imitation of my former self.

At my desk, I scribbled notes documenting as expediently as possible the details of my trip and the massacre of hundreds of Descendants, many of whom were elusive shifters, at the Impresario's gates. We were outmatched. We might as well have been the cultures of folx from the sixteenth century brandishing bows and arrows to ward off Spanish soldiers with their cannons and rifles and horses and dogs. As I scrawled, I wondered more about the briefcase. Tamaya wouldn't have entrusted it to me without cause. I had been so concerned with Lucy and her murdered friends that I had missed Lucy's real intent when she uncuffed the briefcase from my wrist.

The doorbell buzzed, and I jumped from my desk and darted to the door, annoyed that I was disturbed when I was trying to piece together the puzzle before me. I opened the door, slamming it against the wall.

"The heat in my apartment isn't working. Is yours?"

It was Margie, whose age and hair color were as undecipherable as they were unpredictable. Today, her hair was bright pink. It suited her. I had helped her land a coveted job as a researcher at the Grand Library, usually reserved for the young male heirs of Residents, but I claimed Margie could do the grunt work in the basement, filing non-digitized documents in real cardboard boxes. For that she was grateful, and she expressed her gratitude every now and again. Who was I to resist? Although today was inconvenient.

"I don't know. I haven't turned it on."

"Go ask the super. He likes you."

"Ask him what?"

"To turn on the damn heat, Ben. You know he does this every time it gets cold. We have to go begging him, and he won't listen to us plebes, but he likes you. You're a Resident."

She was right. I held enough prestige to convince the nervous guy who was our building manager that it was time to quit saving the oil needed for the antiquated heating system. Unlike other wealthier neighborhoods, our buildings had been constructed with old-fashioned radiators that still operated on oil, and they didn't work without replenishing the boilers as well as maintaining them yearly.

The last time I'd knocked on the iron door to his basement apartment, I heard him unlatching a series of locks, and when he opened the door, he stood out of reach behind burglar bars. He wasn't trustworthy and he didn't like me, but because he mistook my residency at the Grand Library as a link to power, he seemed to grant me a modicum of respect. He had that traumatic unease about him as he fumbled with another bolt on the security bars. Slowly, he unbolted the latch and let me into his cramped basement. He shared the space with a huge combustion chamber, metal tubes, defunct radiators and oil barrels, most of which were empty. I tried to put him at ease as he skulked behind an oil drum. His apartment looked like an explosion waiting to happen.

"It's time to heat the building, Dooley."

"Yeah, I know."

"Well? I have to remind you again? Aren't you going to fire up the boiler?"

"Soon enough." His voice squeaked at a high register and his pointy ears lifted up. "We're running out of oil. And you know, they won't listen to me."

"Put in the request."

"I did," he said. His face flushed, and his ears crinkled up and down when he spoke. "Can you ask them?"

"Again?"

"They listen to you."

"Fine. I'll contact them."

Dooley referred to the local fossil fuel offices run by the oligarchs who manipulated the short supply to their advantage by raising prices at will for profits. One of the Residents at the Library belonged to the global group, and Dooley assumed I could influence him. I couldn't. Instead, I dropped by the district office with fellow Descendants who filled orders and I reminded them to please fill our building's request. In return, they requested books they needed for their secret schools. I didn't ask questions; I just gave them the books.

"HVOs," said Margie. We should have those by now."

"HVOs?"

"Vegetable oil. For heating. You know that hydro whatever process."

"Hydro-treated? Too easy. No one is going to invest in something that isn't going to multiply profits, you know that."

"Yeah. Let's just kill the earth instead, right?"

"Something like that," I said.

Margie walked past me and stood in the middle of my living room filled with boxes of books. I'd lived here for almost a decade and hadn't gotten around to assembling the bookshelves stacked against a wall.

"It's freezing in here too," she said.

Margie untied her hair, and a bright pink copper mane fell past her neck. She was exceedingly attractive and well aware of her beauty.

"You sound different. You seem different too."

She sauntered over to my desk and rifled through my papers. I allowed her curiosity because she often provided commas and sentence structure that I ignored when I wrote hurriedly.

"What's this?" She read out loud.

"How can I become a rebel? I chose to be common. An ordinary idiot. I can't be who I become when I'm with you."

"You're not supposed to read that. It's private," I said.

She ignored me, and I was too embarrassed to show it. If I protested too much, Margie would mock me and not let me forget a second of vulnerability. She read more.

"I've returned with no inkling of where you might be. I pluck from my jacket pocket a poem I wrote, hoping that in the writing of these words you'll intuit across the miles how much I crave your scent. I have a frivolous vestige of you on my flesh. A bruise. Indigo at its center, gradually the bruise transmutes into light mauve with edges a darker russet. Do you remember? You gripped my forearm fiercely. I suppose you surprised yourself, having realized you were on an edge so forlorn you forgot who

you were. Who I was. But I didn't care because your clench sanctified my flesh, and the bruised skin still invokes that grasp. I have proof. See? Here on my left forearm the purple bruise hasn't faded. And when it fades, the flesh will seek you out again. We're both imprinted with deeper scars that either of us can heal."

"Someone's in love," she said.

"Not me," I protested.

"Oh? A casual thing?"

"I didn't say that."

"Sounds like love to me, Ben." She paused and scanned my body. "You look different."

She inched closer and examined my pupils as if searching for something they had once exhibited, and only she and I could detect what that might be. After thorough scrutiny, she stepped back and thrust my letter against my chest. I crumpled the paper with my fist and my face flushed.

"Be careful, Ben."

I looked away and stared out the window.

"Ben? Did you hear me? Be careful. If they know you've been shifting again, they'll find you."

"I don't know what you mean."

"Uh-huh."

"You and your friends shift all the time. Why do you care what I do?"

"Me and my friends are careful." She tossed her hair. "And none of us are kept under observation by your Residents who claim you as their heir and trusted servant." She paused. "Ben. Are you listening?"

I spun around to face her. "Margie, if you were a kid on the streets, where would you live?"

"What?"

"Where would you live?"

"Have you heard anything I've said to you?"

"You must have some idea."

Margie tossed her hair again and twirled the ends of her tresses, resting on one foot then the other, and with each movement her hips rocked.

"Any number of places," she responded.

"The most obvious?" I asked.

"Why?"

"Just curious."

"I know when you're lying."

"Margie," I said firmly. "Where?"

She glared in that way she had about her, suggestive and pensive at once.

"Well, I'd look in alleys."

"But where?"

"Everywhere and anywhere you might see lots of junk. Especially old construction sites."

"That's not very helpful."

"You judge me? Just because I live in these dreaded lofts I'm supposed to know about street kids?"

"Don't you?"

"You found me out."

"Well?"

"Come over, and I'll refresh my memory."

She tripped over a box of books to stand near me, and we caught sight of a hawk circling above a deserted building, crumbling at its core. Hawks often made their nests inside the cavities of a high rise that had been vacated after the last election. That is, if you call vacating being rounded up and sent who knows where. We couldn't be sure, and no one asked, afraid they would be the next to be sent away. More and more hawks and scavengers were inhabiting the city, defying the urban landscape.

PART 3

"I decided then and there that if I was ever free,
I would use my life to uphold the cause of my
sisters and brothers behind walls."
—Angela Davis

"Stay woke, keep their eyes open."
—Lead Belly

LUCY

Lucy was born a Descendant from ocean soul folx that the Ascendant-surveyors proclaimed to be extinct. Of course, they weren't, but the myth of extinction and vanished souls benefitted the Impresario and his henchmen. As a kid, Lucy escaped the suffocation of the camps to wander the streets with others like her. She was one of many with no place to call home.

꩜

"Papi," you say. "Lucy reminded you of me."

"Sometimes."

"I wasn't born yet."

"I know."

"But at that time, she reminded you of me. The daughter you were going to have."

"You're trying to trick me, Yareli."

"Maybe," you respond.

"I don't know about those things."

"What things?"

"The things about time and space and other dimensions that your mother teaches you."

"*Ay*, Papi. Yes, you do know."

"Can I go on, *m'ija*? Please?"

"I'm not stopping you, Papi."

⌒⌒⌒

After Margie's suggestion to look in alleys and construction sites, I found Lucy a few weeks later. At the end of an alley, behind rows and rows of cinder blocks piled one on top of the other, crafting separate private rooms curtained off from a larger common space. I pulled back a thin, yellow paisley ripped curtain that functioned as a door and landed on a pile of filthy, crusty cushions that had once been blue or purple. There she stood.

"You took something from me," I said.

"I did?"

"From the briefcase."

"I did."

Lucy Eufemia reached inside a cubicle made of cinder blocks, extracted the little bomb and placed it in my palm. I inspected the flat, round, silver thing.

"Why'd you take it?" I asked.

"To blast the Impresario's gates, what else?"

"I don't believe you."

I turned the thing over to inspect it further.

"She ordered me to take it," said Lucy.

"Who?"

"Tamaya."

I blinked. "I don't believe you."

"What *do* you believe, Ben?"

She spoke my name like an accusation.

She propped herself against the concrete couch next to me and tapped a rhythm on a thick, cardboard box with both hands. It was a muted sound, but the soft tempo soothed as I assessed the puzzling object in my palm.

"I have to return this."

"Oh, no you don't. We need it."

She leaned closer, snatched the one-inch sized explosive from my palm and returned it to her secret closet behind stacked blocks.

"What are you going to do with it?"

"I told you. We're blasting the Impresario's castle."

"That's a death sentence, Lucy."

"I know. Maybe I don't care."

I looked around her hovel, its dirt floors and cardboard cartons of all sizes that served the dual purpose of tables and drums. The Rebels played trial by fire, experimenting with tactics that assured nothing except more damage. What I realized more and more is that if plans could not be disclosed, it was because no one really knew the plans. They made them up as they went along. Being rogue suited them. In the end, they all wanted the same thing: to bring down the dictator, his White Guards and their impotent lawmakers. But with no real, unified plan, they'd never succeed at anything other than playing at revolution. Looking back, I developed compassion for Lucy, the young Rebel, even though she didn't call herself a "Rebel." I pressed my back against the rigid modules that functioned as a couch or chair.

"We're all gonna die, anyway," Lucy said.

She mumbled and scratched her ear, the left one, the one that maybe warned her when it itched that something wasn't right, but then again, nothing had been right all her life. She was born into calamitous times that held children and youths as hostages. They had no future. They only had the moment to live to the fullest, and the fullest meant blasting the White Guards and global dictators to hell. All to hell.

"And these assholes," she mumbled. "I don't mean the White Guards or the ASSES or the Impresario, 'cause we all know they're fucking assholes. I mean, the Rebels and Tamaya and now you." She looked at me with disdain. "You aren't gonna do shit for us. I'm fifteen years old, and this is the only fucked up world I've ever known. Massacres of Descendants like me. That's every fucking day. Nobody cares. Tamaya just pretends to care, but she's no different from all the Rebels who think they're the second or third coming of some shithead messiah. I hate them all. Except América. She's the only one who watches out for us. Us younger folx, the ones who live in our concrete dumps, we take care of each other because we're nothing but pawns to those Rebels who follow Tamaya. They say they care what happens to us, but they don't give a rat's ass. I bet a rat's ass could care for us more than they do."

Lucy stumbled around, speaking louder and angrier. She kicked at the gray bricks and a few tumbled, causing a gaping hole to the outside alley.

"I mean, if you think about the fact that rat's poop-shit pebbles out of their ass, then you'd know that's what they think of us. Like we can be swept away and thrown in the garbage. Just like that. We don't mean more than shit to the Impresario and the White Guard, and we mean even less than shit to the Rebels. We don't have any fucking heroes. Fuck, we've never had any fucking heroes, not in my fifteen years of life."

Lucy bent down and stretched her arm through the hollow she'd created, and one by one, she gathered the blocks and plugged the hole. She griped louder and louder and spit from her mouth driveled to the dirt floor. Her chest swelled and she pressed her hand against it as if to calm her anxiety. Pausing for a second, she breathed in long and gently to slacken the discomfort that could easily debilitate her if she wasn't careful. She whispered, I suspect, because whispers often clung like prayers that eased the twinge in her chest. At least, that's how I calmed myself.

"Papi, why are you making up things about Lucy?"

"What makes you think I'm making things up, Yareli?"

You shake your head and return to your journal. You might be taking notes. I hope you are. What I won't say is that I want to make Lucy come alive for you and so I expand what I may not understand but what I think I see.

I continue.

"Tears streamed down Lucy's cheeks.

"All I'd ever known or seen was god-awful shit with Descendants pretending to be who they weren't and hating on us folx because we weren't the right kind of Descendants. They think because they bow down to another kinda god that they know more than we do. Pretending to wanna save us and using us like bait for their rat traps. And us shifters? Us soul folx? We have to hide. Nobody likes us . . . well, except for the fuckers like the Impresario and his mighty fucked up friends. Yeah, everybody likes a shifter at night or in some dark corner where nobody sees them with us."

She rubbed her tears hard and soiled her cheeks into shiny brown. "I'm not stupid. I caught on to the only game in town. Run jobs for the Rebels. That's what the older kids told us. My buddies, Kim, Birdy and Padma, they watched out for us and said, 'Yeah, you can trust that one over there but don't get caught up in her meet-ups 'cause she'll run you to the ground.' That's what they said about Tamaya the Rebel Warrior. Well, FUCK YOU, Tamaya Rebel Warrior!" Finally, she turned and looked me in the eye. "And fuck you too!"

"I'm sorry, Lucy."

She grinned. "Sure you are."

"I am. I wish things were different. I do." I paused. "Now, please let me have that thing."

"What thing?"

"The bomb."

"Bomb? You think it's a bomb?

"Isn't it?"

Okay, maybe it is and maybe it isn't. Maybe it's just a thing to distract all you assholes."

"Call it what you want. Just give it here and I'll return it to the briefcase for safe keeping."

"Not a good idea," she said.

"Why not?"

"Not a good idea," she repeated.

She winked at me and grinned again, this time, somewhat sincerely.

"You know the school I went to?"

"No, I don't. I didn't know you went to school."

"'Cause it was a prison. Me and my class buddies called it 'the Prison.' Well, most mornings, I was late to class even though our dorms were close by. Those damn dorms had about twenty twin beds, rickety and old, in each room. More like cots with stinky, old mattresses made of foam. I never really could sleep at night, so I'd sneak out and walk. Just walk by myself in the woods. Felt peaceful. Sometimes I'd get caught slipping out, they'd punish me, but I was used to it. You know, beatings with leather straps if the preceptor wanted to give somebody a beating that day."

Lucy stretched her hand down her back and pulled up her thin blouse to expose the welts and bumps on her brown flesh. The scars adorned her spine with knots that unfolded and looped into vines.

I winced and quickly looked away.

"Like I said, I was late to class most mornings. A lousy history class, anyway, and that fool only went on and on about wars that didn't matter anymore. Not like he ever taught about the Woke Wars, you know?

"I'd walk in and he'd stare at the clock on the wall, an old digital clock, and he'd say, 'Late again, Lucy Eufemia,' and I swear it was barely three minutes. That's all. Just three minutes. 'I'll have to report you to the office,' he'd say and then I'd sit down bored as fuck, but he didn't stop there. He'd pick on me. Call on me to see if I had the answers to his stupid bullshit questions about some Great War and another called the Good War from so fucking long ago, who cares? I mean, how can wars be great or good? Sometimes, I'd get him back and ask, 'What about the Woke Wars? Why don't you talk about the Woke Wars? From the 60s?' 'Those are all myths,' he'd say. Those were riots, not wars, and certainly not legal protests. Just riots that your kind started. And you know it's illegal to talk about those myths,' he'd say. I wouldn't stop. I'd keep badgering the old guy, 'But if they're myths, aren't they just stories? Aren't you teaching us stories about your wars? Why don't you tell us about the stories that started all the woke stuff?'

"That really pissed him off but I didn't care. Not one bit. And the next morning, I'd be late again. And again, he'd stare up at that digital clock, and say to me, 'You're late, Lucy Eufemia. I'll have to report you to the office.' And he'd report me for being three lousy minutes late, and eventually I'd get punished again. Got plenty of scars to prove it too."

Lucy sat on the crusty cushions, her head resting on her knees. I heard her breath soft and cadenced, as if she was comforting herself. She stared up at me and I saw tears welling up. She turned her head away from me and wiped her face with the hem of her shirt.

"We're heroes. Me and my friends. And you, you're just like Tamaya. And the rest of them," she whispered. "Here," she held up the bombing device. "Take it, you know you don't need it. Not like we do."

I nodded and left empty-handed.

AMÉRICA

I left Lucy's cinder block castle and returned to my loft
apartment, sad for Lucy and her friends and yet, fully aware I
was powerless to help them. I was as much of a pawn as they
were. I had just made myself a cup of tea, when I heard keys rattling at my front door. It was América.

"You have keys to my apartment?" I asked.

"Ah, Ben. Why wouldn't I have keys?"

And by that I'm sure she meant she had bribed the building's Superintendent, who was hardly if ever around when we
needed him. For bribes, he was readily available.

"What do you want, América?"

"To seduce you," she said.

"Seduce me? You had a chance on the island."

"Not while Tamaya was indoctrinating you."

"Is that what it's called?"

"Call it what you want. You're ours now."

"I don't know what you mean."

"You hurt me, Ben."

"I have no idea what you're talking about."

But I did. I knew.

≈≈≈

"Papi, why did you pretend?"

"Pretend?"

"That you didn't know her?"

"Did I say I didn't know her?"

"Never mind."

⮜⮜⮜

Years earlier, when I happened upon América, I was at a production of *El Divino Narciso* by the acclaimed seventeenth-century poet, writer, philosopher, nun Sor Juana Inés de la Cruz. My mothers had insisted I become an avid reader of the nun's poetry. This particular *loa*, or short play, "The Divine Narcissus," was esteemed because the allegorical characters symbolically represent the Spanish colonizers and the not yet colonized Indigenous. For me, the play centers on América, the fierce Indigenous woman who refuses to give up her spiritual beliefs and culture.

I sat in the fifth row on the left side of the ragged public theater, watching rats run back and forth at the hem of the curtains. And when I say rats, I mean germ-infested creatures the size of racoons wandering through filthy parts of the city. The curtain had yet to rise, emboldening a pedant sitting next to me to warble inanely about Sor Juana's literature. I was thrilled when a somewhat leggy, ample woman stumbled through the row of patrons and ordered him to move. Her curly hair was cropped close to her head, and I couldn't help but notice the constellation of moles steering my gaze from the corner of her red lips up past her flush nose to the mole below her left eye. I stared because she was more than beautiful. She was familiar.

"Let me guess. América is your favorite character," she said.

Her eyes shimmered hazel, reminding me of a cat that loitered in my apartment's hallway, then disappeared after I became dependent on feeding him.

"An easy guess. She's everyone's favorite," I said.

"It's rare to find a man not threatened by a woman's intellect." I nodded.

"I'm América."

"América? Like the character? In the play?"

She was silent for a moment. "They call me América."

"That's not really your name?" I asked.

"Maybe."

"The secrets begin."

"We all had secrets. At the camps. You remember?"

I must have looked dumbfounded.

"Remember?" she asked again.

She repositioned herself on the moth-ridden seat, tossed her head back to gaze at the ceiling and announced, "You said you loved me."

The surrounding patrons gawked as if to accuse me of being a derelict father who had abandoned his wife and children to pursue an ambition that matched a modern-day Lothario's. Instantly, I felt guilty for having wronged the woman sitting next to me, who I thought I'd just met. I studied her fleshy nose and sphere-shaped eyes with dark, dense eyelashes. I dug deep into my memory and had no recollection. She reached for my hand and pressed my fingers against the back of her head bordering the neck's nape, shielded by thick curls of hair. My index finger circled a round bump, and I tugged her head nearer to examine a brown mole. I had stroked this mole on a boy I had known in a work camp with four hundred other children.

"Dredge up any memories?" she asked.

I bowed my head. "Marco?"

I fell silent, and my stomach churned, prompting the ulcers from those years at the camps to twinge.

"We were friends," she said.

"I know," I mouthed.

I sank forward and rested my forehead on my hands.

"Until that day," she said.

I nodded and coughed. My throat coarse, as if stuffed with cotton balls, and I coughed louder. América smiled. When I couldn't catch my breath, she slapped my back, grabbed my arms and lifted them in the air.

"You're still doing that," she said. "Making yourself choke."

I gasped for breath. "It was my fault . . . that they took you."

I bent down and put my head between my knees to stop coughing.

EXPERIMENTS

I was a changed Benito in the camps, unafraid of shifting, just like Marco had taught me. He had been fearless each time we met at midnight in a shrouded corner beside a muddy pond.

"On your thirtieth birthday . . . we'll celebrate. You'll be Alejandra. Not Benito. Not anymore."

"That's a long time from now," I said.

"Only eighteen years."

"And you?"

"I'll find you."

"What if I don't want to be found?" I asked.

Marco outstretched his taut, sable-brown body on the frayed cotton sheets we'd stolen from our mattresses. We lay there studying the moonlit clouds that reminded us of cadavers. He leaned in, breathed on my neck and kissed my lips. When I reached up to kiss him, he transmuted to a female body, full and delicious, while I consciously held back and sustained my male physique. We did this often—practiced transmutations that desire dictated during our secret meetings. We didn't question or judge, and when he renamed me, I felt free in ways I couldn't explain. Marco would always be Marco. But I was wrong.

～⌒～⌒～

"Papi, I'm confused. So América was Marco?"

"Yes," I replied.

"And Marco was América?"

"Yareli, I thought you already knew this."

"I just wanna be sure, Papi."

"Haven't you been listening?"

"I've been listening."

"How many times have we gone over these stories I tell you?"

"I don't know. Lots and lots of times, I guess."

"I guess you don't always listen, huh? Is that what you're telling me?"

"I listen, Papi. Sometimes, the stories are hard. Like when you talk about the experiments. But I gotta hear that too."

"Why?" I ask.

"'Cause they happened, that's why."

I'm silent.

"Say what they did. The experiments," you beg me.

⌁⌁⌁

I don't answer you. I can't. But I realize I have to repeat this part if only for myself because I still can't grasp it all. I often thought I'd dreamed the nightmare about orphans in those so-called recreational camps that the Impresario and his band of wealthy, vile men made for children and adolescents without parents. I had assumed my birth parents were dead. That's what we were told. Ever since I could remember, I had been at camps with hundreds of others like me. That's where I met Marco.

He was swimming with other black and brown kids. Near the pond, a thick rope drooped from a sycamore tree, and I spotted him swinging through the air with his legs wrapped around the line. As he swung into the deep end, he jumped and splashed everyone. Children screamed and giggled. For a sweet moment, I thought this camp might be different. He popped up from the depths, and the kids encircled him shrieking and splashing water. Marco stumbled to a sandy bank, fell and rested on his elbows, tossing back his black ringlets. He motioned to me to join him, and I shied away, but my legs stepped in his direction, and I sat down beside him on the sand.

"You're the new kid," he said.

My eyes watered. I had been transferred from another site where a friend of mine had died, they said, from yet another variant of a global virus. Marco set his hand on my shoulder and, when one of the White Guards lifted his rifle and pointed the barrel at me, Marco shoved me aside and shielded my body with his. The guard chuckled, lowered the weapon and leaned it against his leg. This camp was no different.

Marco and I became inseparable. Most days we swam together in the pond not far from the tin buildings where we slept and ate and did everything the White Guards instructed. We kept to ourselves while the guards kept firm watch, stalking the kids they favored, saving them for their harrowing experiments.

One day, Marco and I peeked inside a window, painted over in green, where we found a clear crack in a lower corner. We balanced on bricks and took turns peeking. I only glanced twice because I couldn't stomach what I saw and was afraid that the more I looked, the more likely they'd do it to me and to Marco. The guards had a kid shifting on a slab of metal in the middle of the room, where they got on top of her and started doing things to her. Ugly sex things that she didn't want but, soon enough, she'd shift and become a boy with boy genitals. Then, they'd turn him over and someone else would get on the slab and do ugly sex things, and the boy's genitals would shift back to girl genitals. The White Guards would repeat it again and again. The guards prodded and poked to see how many times they could get a shifter to transmute in an hour. But shifting was painful when you weren't ready and didn't feel like transmuting.

Marco and I rarely shifted more than once in one night because, while it felt good at first, too much back and forth when you weren't used to it caused pain. But the guards forced the transmutations, and the coercion was agonizing. We saw tears rolling down the faces of the kids on the slab. As Marco spied, his face grew red and he smacked his fist hard into his other hand. I mouthed to him that we had to go, but he couldn't stop watching. Finally, I dragged him down, and the bricks we stood on crashed loudly.

That's when a guard ran to the window and opened it, but I had already hustled around the corner. Not Marco. He faced the guard head on. Another guard came outside and grabbed him. He didn't scream or fight. He knew what was coming. I never forgave myself . . . for running. But I blamed him for his carelessness.

A week later, I snuck into to his cell while the guards played their daily poker, making bets on which Descendant shifters could be tamed easier. I slipped past their recreation room that served as kitchen and dining area as well and grabbed a keycard hanging from the open door. When I reached Marco's cell, I pointed the card at a digital screen and the door unlocked. Marco was shackled to an iron bed frame, his wrists and ankles restrained in steel manacles.

"Get the fuck out of here before they trap you too," said Marco.

"I wanted to see you," I said.

"You've seen me. Now go."

"Are you okay?"

"Oh yeah, I'm doing great, Ben."

I looked down at the concrete floor, rank with blood and vomit. "I have to get you out of here."

Marco laughed. "Come here," he said, angling his head up.

When I inched closer to his face, close enough for his breath to puff on my mouth, I kissed him, and he bit my bottom lip so brutally I tasted blood. I jerked back and must have looked stunned, but his face was blank. Unfeeling. I shuffled out of the room, walking backwards, wanting his expression to flash a speck of emotion, but he stared coldly, his eyes dim and hollow.

Even when he was cruel, I couldn't stop loving him, but if my body ever roused an inkling of a memory about Marco, I abruptly stuffed it back into a dead zone. I reasoned that love happens, then it's gone for whatever reason, floating into another realm to embrace someone or something else. I tossed Marco into a past life that I never wanted in my present.

In retrospect, when I chose to be Ben, unwilling to shift, he began to despise me. And yet here we were. Marco, now América, challenging me to become the person they believed in: Alejandra, the warrior for nothing and no one.

⤙⤙⤙

"Papi, you're too hard on yourself," you say.
"*M'ija*, I speak my truth."
I continue.

FORGIVENESS

From the couch, América lifted her chin, commanding me to join her. I placed the tea on the table in front of her and returned to the kitchen to make myself another cup. I watched as she sipped the beverage. Her lips puckered on the edge of the teacup and, as she sipped, she pursed them around its edges and slurped noisily without caring who or what might hear, as if to say, "Fuck you all and your petty rules about decorum. We come from the land of fucked-up camps where you placed us as if we weren't human. So, I'm sure as fuck not gonna act human whatever the fuck human is for you."

I admired that about her, even though she frightened me.

"You want another cup?" I asked.

She shook her head.

I sat down next to her, and her hand grazed the naked flesh of my arm.

My body tingled and burned the way it did when she was near. Even when I denied feelings, my skin seared. She leaned in, took my cup, swallowed the tea, returned the cup to the table and with warm lips kissed my neck.

"Please don't," I mumbled.

"Alejandra, Alejandra, Alejandra," she breathed on my flesh. "When will you stop lying to yourself?"

Maybe it was the way she sighed with curious longing or maybe it was my own yearning. I tried to push it all away, but I craved the sting of her touch. When she was near, my flesh could not be trusted. When she was near like this, unguarded, América the Rebel softened. Without much predisposition, I shifted into Alejandra, and América's lips no longer grazed my neck. She was, as usual, full of surprises.

"Where is it?" she asked.

"Don't do that."

"What?"

"Please. Don't disappear like that."

"Fuck, Alejandra. What do you want from me?"

"Forgiveness"

"Forgive you? For what?"

"You're right. I can't forgive you either."

América was silent.

"It wasn't my fault you ended up strapped to a table at the camp," I said.

"It wasn't my fault you were in the bathroom that day," she said.

Now I was silent.

"But you got your revenge, didn't you? And all you had to do was stand by. Do nothing. That's who you are, right? Innocently standing by while others take the fall."

I grabbed her wrist and drew her to me. "Please, let's not do this. Not now."

She laid her head on mine, and I palmed her forehead, dabbing her eyelids. I trekked below her eye to her nose, sketching the contours of black, oval birthmarks.

"I never stopped, you know," she said.

"Stopped?"

"Loving you. And that pisses me off."

My finger wandered up her cheek, roaming on charted beauty marks. "I never stopped either."

"Stopped what? Say it."

"Like the song says, 'I've been loving you so long, I can't stop now.'"

"Like the other song says, 'love has no pride,'" she responded.

"And let's not forget, 'love is stronger than pride.'"

"But that's not always true. In our case."

"What do you mean?"

"How long since you've seen me?"

"How long since you've seen *me*?" I asked.

"That's my point exactly, Alejandra. Pride has been guiding you. You stayed away."

"I stayed away because I loved you, love you."

"Yeah, right."

She looked up at the ceiling, seemingly counting the gray panels above us. Then, she brushed my lips with her fingers and tapped two fingers in slow rhythm on my lower lip, acknowledging the scar she'd left behind like a trophy, a reminder that claimed me as hers.

"It's okay. It's over. We're here now and we have things to do," she said.

"Like?"

"Close down the camps. Save the kids like us."

"That's impossible."

"Is it? We've been doing it. One by one. You just don't hear about it. Did you really trust that *The Hungry Hawk* would report about the camps we've blown up? And the kids we've saved from those camps? And I don't mean the ones that can leave when they want. Like you did."

"I didn't leave when I wanted to."

"Didn't you? Your mothers adopted you. And you left. Cozy and free."

"I thought everyone was going to be adopted."

"Yeah, well, you're a fool, Alex. You knew what was happening in those rooms. They weren't going to let us go. We served a purpose. We were branded."

"But you got out," I reminded her.

"I escaped. With Tamaya's help. And the Rebels. It's what they do. It's what we do. I thought Tamaya explained this to you."

"She never explained anything to me. When I told her I wanted to help, she scorned me."

"Scorned you?"

"Scorned me."

América chuckled. "That mission is already underway."

"Why couldn't she tell me?"

She shrugged her shoulders. "You know Tamaya. Full of mystery." She raised her eyebrows and widened her eyes, mocking Tamaya's earnestness, or so it seemed.

"What's up with you two?" I asked.

"Nothing. Why?"

"You slammed her hard. On the island."

"You saw that?"

"You know I did."

"What I want to know is why you didn't join me. In the water."

"You knew I followed you?"

"Of course, I knew. You wanted me to know."

"Hence, the show. Thank you for that, by the way."

"Just like old times," she said. "At the camp."

She jiggled her head and reviewed the ceiling panels again. "Wild nights, wild nights, wild, wild horses," she said. "That's what it was like. That's who we were. Some things I don't regret."

She focused on the ceiling, pausing to consider her next statement.

"That day . . . at the theater . . . you ran out, remember? Made up some sorry-ass excuse. What was it? You left beans cooking on your stove, or some shit like that? And you didn't leave your number, your address, nothing."

"You knew where to find me," I said.

"Yeah. I also knew you didn't want to be found. You've been lost. So far away from me. From us."

"You were living your revolution. You didn't need me."

"But I wanted you. And I missed you. Every day, Alejandra. I missed you. And you ran. From you. And who you were becoming. I told Tamaya to go get you at the Grand Library. Did you know that? I was sure she could lure *el gran* Ben Espinoza. You're so damn predictable."

América tugged me close to her mouth. We kissed, and I tried to remember why I had left her. I didn't want those all-too-common sentiments, the passion that lies, the sensation that subsides. Not again. Because even though she said I ran, América ran faster and farther. Wild horses, all right. And I couldn't trust her. But here I was in her embrace again, waiting for the other proverbial shoe to drop, because it would. I'd made my peace with those early years at the camp. At least I thought I had. But when she flaunted what I couldn't resist, I slid into an abyss of my own making. And yet, Tamaya lured me in, too. Both had manipulated me, and I applauded their scheming, even though they pissed me off for keeping secrets. I sat up abruptly and shoved América's head off my lap. She frowned at me, eyes narrowed, and rose from the couch.

"Fuck you," she said.

"Yeah. Fuck me."

Unsettled, she paced the floor. "Fine. Okay. Well, where is it?"

I motioned with my chin so faintly, even I didn't know what I meant.

"Where?" she repeated.

I sank further into the cushion. "I don't know what you want," I said.

América rummaged through the drawers of a side table.

"You know that feeling when you assume someone is going to slap you?" I asked. "All day long you sense the sting creeping closer and closer."

She tossed items from a drawer to the floor. Scarves, mittens, keys from who knows what, even lipstick I'd never seen before. América grabbed the lipstick cylinder, removed the cap and held it up to the sunlight. The faded rose shade caught her attention briefly, until she flung the lipstick and it rolled against a book box, smearing the tile floor with rose strips.

"It's a sensation that the body's memory anticipates, and the mind refuses the memory, but the body insists and the hurt looms. The physical pain is near, and flesh is so imprinted that it expects pain because flesh doesn't want to be fooled again."

I studied the ceiling. Cobwebs in the corner between two walls and the ceiling. "A peculiar response, huh? I mean, just now, in this body as Alejandra, the sensations are vivid again."

"Where the fuck is it, Alex?"

"And there's a point when you welcome the slap, not because you crave that physical pain, but because you want the anticipation to end. You want to relax into yourself without having to obsess about the slap that's coming. When it's here finally, when the slap or the punch or the grip finally lands, the body doesn't feel the wound because the mind is relieved it's done. For today, it's done. Until tomorrow.

"Do you remember that feeling, América? In the camps?"

She yanked open the bottom drawer on the table beside the couch, and more items spilled to the floor. América kicked and smashed everything that rolled out. A part of me enjoyed watching her impatience, but despite my apprehension about what we had meant to each other, I was more curious that, as Alejandra, my senses swelled, intensifying the body's veiled imprints, with each new shift. What a stereotype, I thought. Feminine intuition.

"Lucy has it," I said.

"You idiot. How could you let her take it?"

"How could I know she had taken what I didn't even know I had?"

América tensed her mouth and held her breath. "Fine. Let's go."

"Why do you need me to go?" I asked.

"I don't."

WOKE WARS (W5)

On our way to Lucy's cinder block dwelling, we stopped at a local market, which were scarce on the side of town that Descendant soul folx inhabited. Most of the well-stocked markets with fresh food were closer to the Impresario's compound, with one or two superstores near the Residents' neighborhoods. This market had survived because locals trusted the owners, who allowed customers to run a tab, fully aware of their erratic employment.

América purchased eggs, fresh basil, tomatoes, garlic and pasta, filling up a burlap sack that she deposited in my hands.

"Planning a party?" I asked.

She fed Lucy's pack, most of whom had almost no means for nutritious food. The adolescents were either from northern camps trained to be clerks servicing the wealthy in department stores, banks and such, or they were from southern camps targeted to be janitors, field workers and the like. Each camp placed a select few shifters in bordellos, where they were imprisoned after the horrific experiments in the camps had wrung out their will to live. Whether from the north or south, the young soul folx who escaped from their assigned prisons hid in plain sight, and nobody cared what became of them so long as they stayed out of sight. They created these cinder block communities they called home.

América drew back the yellow paisley curtain and bent her head to enter Lucy's cubicle. I followed behind. Lucy hovered over an electric hot plate, stirring a mixture that smelled of dead skunk.

"Throw that mess away," said América.

Lucy grinned a foolish, crooked grin, and ran into América's outstretched arms and clung to her.

"You're back," she said.

"I always come back," said América. "Let me look at you."

She stepped back to hold Lucy at arm's length, and I found myself mimicking their smiles.

Lucy glared at me.

"You've met Alejandra?" América asked.

"I've met Ben."

She snatched the sack of food from me and set it on a rusty aluminum table she'd probably found in one of the garbage piles that lined the streets. She plucked from the sack the dry noodles and vegetables and yelled out, "Looks like we're having spaghetti tonight."

Eight scraggly folx scuttled in from their cubicles, hungry and eager. Immediately, América started chopping tomatoes, garlic and basil and tossing them into a tin pot with olive oil.

"Why are *they* here?" Lucy asked, pointing at me.

"Alex is here to learn," said América.

"Learn? Learn what?"

"Whatever she can."

To appear less conspicuous, I backed away from the cooking area and found a corner. América rummaged beneath a makeshift plywood shelf held up by blocks on each end and pulled out a bent container with a hole in the bottom. She held it up and looked at Lucy, who scrunched up her shoulders as she listened to a pair of neighbors quarrel about the deaths of close friends. América pulled out a ceramic crock from beneath the shelf, paused and fiddled with a device between her thumb and forefinger. I stared at the coin-shaped explosive, and Lucy widened her eyes at América, who was listening intently to her friends' debate.

"Birdy and Kim were dumbasses," said a girl. "They shoulda listened to Padma. They all got blown up because they didn't listen."

"Fuck that," answered a young white boy, probably fourteen or so, named Coltrane. "It was Padma who went out on her own and didn't listen to the plan. If she had, they'd all be sitting here right now with us."

"That's bullshit, and you know it, Coltrane," said Lucy. "We went over that plan again and again, but they thought they knew better and took off on their own, wanting to show off like they were heroes. Well, who the fuck is the hero now?"

"Don't get mad at me!" said Coltrane.

Coltrane had a skinny, pale frame and chestnut hair tangled in back and long in front. With thin fingers, he brushed aside bangs that hid his brown eyes. He stumbled when a tall boyish girl with a shaved head shoved him aside to inch up next to Lucy. I stared and realized she, or he, might have really been a girlish boy named Z. Just Z. Z squeezed in on a bench and spoke with more authority than Lucy, who was not bossed by anybody. Not by América and certainly not by me.

"The thing is," said Z, "none of that matters. We lost three good Rebels, and now it's up to us, and let me tell you, it's not gonna be easy."

Z proceeded to pull clusters of wrapped chocolates and gummies from cargo pants and tossed the sweets onto the concrete slab that served as a table.

"All for love," Z said.

At nineteen, Z was the oldest of the group gathered that evening in Lucy's cubicle. I recognized faces from the café and, like carbon copies, they were massacred for the cause, always more materializing like a never-ending supply. After mourning their losses, they'd gather courage and devise another plan. That was all they knew. All they had ever known. These kids, these children, were raised in a Global Order with an Impresario who had instigated havoc in their lives, and havoc was all they understood.

"We will win the Woke Wars," yelled Coltrane. He cast his fist in the air, and others joined in as they chanted their slogan.

"You idiots don't even know why they're called the Woke Wars," said Lucy.

"Sure, we do," answered Coltrane. "It's all about Malcom X, and the Black Panthers, and Angela Davis, and the Brown Berets, and César Chávez, and. . . ."

"And don't forget Stonewall," said Z. "Don't forget Marsha P. Johnson. And Sylvia Rivera."

"What about WARN, Women of All Red Nations with Madonna Thunder Hawk. Everybody forgets about WARN," said Coltrane. "They were on the frontlines at Alcatraz."

"And Wounded Knee," said Z. "With Mary Crow Dog and Leonard Crow Dog."

"How do you know all this?" I asked.

Z and Coltrane ignored me. Lucy looked at me and clenched her jaw. Finally, acknowledgment from Lucy.

Coltrane punched the air with his fist and chanted, "We will win the Woke Wars!"

⌁⌁⌁

"Papi, why?"

"Why?" I glance at you. You haven't looked up from your journal, where you seem to be sketching an equation or a loop theory your mother taught you.

"Do you mean, why did the young Rebels fight for a hopeless cause?" I ask.

"It wasn't hopeless, Papi."

Your focus is precise, your equation exact. I have no idea what you're hypothesizing.

"Life is full of contradictions, *m'ija*."

"*Ay*, Papi." You shake your head, fixed on your theory.

"Calculating?" I ask.

You lift your head and peer at me. "Did Mami know?"

"Know?"

"About you and América."

I shake my head hesitantly and shrug my shoulders. You nod and return to calculations that will impress your mother. I envy the knowledge you share and revel in your precision. It's getting late, although with no windows and only artificial lighting, we can't chart the revolving treks of the moon and sun. Only on days when we're shoved to outdoor grounds to walk in circles or witness a recent horror do we realize that evening is falling. I sense an inner clock I attribute to perceptions that evolve from shifting. Intuition grows stronger by the day. You were born with clairvoyance, while I attempt to transcend senses that no longer serve me.

"Well?" you ask.

"Oh, you want me to continue?"

But I'm interrupted. The cries of a baby in the next cage grow louder. A girl, probably eight or nine years old, holds the baby close to her chest and rocks back and forth on the floor of the icy concrete. The baby is hungry, cold and ill. In that pen, only children under twelve are confined. Your mother and the other Descendant women rise and walk to the end of our enclosure that faces the one with the children. Some of the women bang their fists against the steel, while others pull and push on the webbed fence. Some chant a prayer and shout for the guards to assist the baby. A pallid-skinned adolescent, who is a White Guard, emerges from behind iron double doors, unbolts the cage, snatches the baby and disappears behind the doors at the end of the hallway. The cinnamon girl who had held the baby, is whimpering, and repeating, "*Por favor, cuida a mi hermanita,*" but the baby will die within days or hours. There's no medicine, no doctors, no milk and no water to cleanse the child.

The coarseness with which the White Guard has seized the infant makes you tremble. You place your hands over your ears as you watch dutifully. Your hypersensitivity to loud noise has afflicted you since you were a baby. But your sensitivities drive you to intuit things outside our cage. The Descendant women with Tamaya hum more prayers, aware of what is to come. The death of brown and black children is of no consequence to our captors, and in fact, the guards accelerate the deaths by placing the children in freezing lock-ups with no blankets. They quarantine the recent arrivals in the refrigerated storage bins to protect us from the latest virus, they say, but they don't care about the viruses spreading among us.

I see tears on your cheeks. You get up and walk to the edge of our coop and poke a finger through the wire and call out to the cinnamon girl. When the girl doesn't acknowledge you, you whistle softly, and she lifts her head toward you, paces closer and pokes her finger through the wire.

I wipe my cheeks, hoping you won't see the tears. I have to practice courage in your presence. I have to go on.

ALEJANDRA

The following day, I went to the café. I wasn't sure why, except for the fact that I was shunned by América and Lucy, who sent me on my way without any hint of their next insurrection. I suspected they didn't need me anymore. I'd served my purpose as a courier.

I took comfort from the aroma of garlic and cumin and, in my own way, waited for Tamaya, because there was no point in searching. I returned daily for a week but found no Tamaya nor América and, although I knew where to locate Lucy, I chose to stay away. I was in limbo, at an impasse, existing on an edge of nothingness. Sorry for myself.

Without any of these so-called Rebel friends, nostalgia for the Grand Library flooded my otherwise lively temperament. It was time to do what I'd been avoiding. When I entered the marble foyer, Head Resident Augustus Marcus scanned my muscular arms and perky breasts.

"A careless end to an otherwise promising career, Resident Espinoza."

"Let me explain," I replied.

How could I explain who I felt myself becoming? In many ways, even as Alejandra, I was still a Resident, and yet I wasn't. I had become an in-betweener flanked by who I had been and who I was becoming. I wasn't surprised when Augustus Marcus handed me a key card and said, "Gather your materials, Miss Espinoza. Or we'll burn them."

The key card opened the ornate wooden door that led to my desk. Piled high were my notes and an array of books I'd been cramming before Tamaya had disrupted a life now undone. Beneath a cluttered pile of loose papers, I spotted a clean, white envelope that I didn't recognize. I picked up the sealed, rectangular envelope seemingly light and empty. I dropped into my desk chair, head bowed and looked around the room, somewhat paranoid that the Residents were tracking my every move. I slipped the blade of a letter opener between the gluey casings and found a handwritten note that said, "Look behind you." Too suspicious to fall into a trap, I refused to turn around and instead got up and went around to the front of my desk and bent down as if to pick up something I'd dropped. When I stood up, I saw nothing and no one who might have ordered me to look into the void of my once precious archive.

"Is there a problem?" Augustus Marcus asked, sticking his head into the room.

I quickly stepped back behind my desk and shuffled papers to cover the note.

"You do realize you no longer have privileges here, Miss Espinoza."

I jumbled up more papers. "Dr. Espinoza," I replied.

"You have until the end of the day, *Miss* Espinoza," he said.

I suppose I should have been sad or angry, anything but the momentary paranoia resulting from the cryptic note. Without really caring, I swiveled in my chair to face the middle of the room, wondering if anyone would show themselves as the author of the message. Perhaps a Resident was playing me for a fool, joking with me, and had left the envelope to dupe me or to torment me simply because he could. Did I regret who and what I had become? A revolutionary shifter? A Rebel no longer in disguise? Fuck all of you, I thought, but I didn't think it at all. I yelled the words so clearly that two guards hastened from out of nowhere, grabbed my arms, dragged me out of the room and tossed me into the street, out of my beloved Grand Library. Not so beloved anymore. I had nowhere else to go. Suddenly, emptiness consumed me. I sat down on the asphalt curb and buried my head between my knees.

"Who sent the note, Papi?"

"You know who sent it."

You're quiet, then reply, "You think it was me, don't you?"

"Wasn't it?"

Again, you're pensive as you devise theorems and diagrams in your journal.

"What were you studying?" you ask.

"Huh?"

"What were you writing? At the Library?"

"Nothing important."

"Didn't the Library study time travel?"

"Time travel? No such thing."

The look on your face surprises me, but then again, it doesn't. You're disappointed. I'm not the rebel or revolutionary others had made me out to be. In my reciting this story repeatedly, you recognize the self-serving fool I had once been. I'm ashamed of my past. I want to cry but I can't. All I have ever lived for, began to live for, was to impress you and your mother and to love you both beyond measure. And I did. But before you entered my life, I had hidden myself from all I could be and might become. When fear drives a coward, the comfort of complacency is just enough. That's all. It's just enough.

COUNSELORS AND INTERROGATIONS

It's morning, and we've all slept through the night without too much disruption after the baby was seized from her sister. Another day, and we'll all try to forget the previous one, because only in forgetting will we find hope, the hope and fortitude to escape.

I'm exhausted. I see you sleeping, and I adjust your shredded cotton blanket over your shoulders. Your eyelids crinkle, the edges curve.

"It's time, Papi. Remember, don't change the story. They get suspicious."

It is time. The Counselors, that is, the Impresario's henchmen, will probe me again, anticipating lies, coaxing misinformation to give them a reason to transfer me to another site—one without children or family members.

An adolescent White Guard bangs on the cage, and I want to scream at him to be quiet, aware that if I scream, there will be consequences.

"Let's go," he yells, banging louder on the fence, obviously to wake up the entire compound.

I place my hands over your ears, and you push them away. I stumble to the steel cage door and the guard slaps me from behind and pokes his nightstick in the small of my back.

In the cubicle, a lightbulb dangles from the ceiling. I sit on a dented aluminum chair with stains that might be congealed blood. The blots are dark brown and crusty at the edges. Something is different, or at least my stomach churns in expectation, and that intuitive part of me that had been coalescing comes alive. I lean back on the fragile frame, trying not to tip it over, but the chair's back legs slip, and I topple to the concrete floor. I touch the blood on the back of my head. I've bitten my tongue. Fingers tap my shoulder, and an arm extends to lift me up. It's Resident Cicero.

"Don't be so shocked, my friend," he says.

"And yet, I am."

"I've been sent."

"To cheer me up?"

"You do have a flair for the dramatic. Nevertheless . . ."

The guard squeezes a high back leather chair into the room. Cicero sits down, crosses one leg over the other and props his back against the supple leather with the ease of an autocrat about to light an expensive cigar.

"We have a proposition for you."

"Sounds ominous."

"We want you to come back to the Grand Library."

"We? Who is *we*?"

"The Residents voted. They agreed you're being held unfairly, well, that is, they voted and concluded you've been duped and that you should return as the heretical Benito Espinoza, of course. You wouldn't be allowed in as you are now."

Cicero scans my physique and gawks at my breasts.

"I wouldn't? But why not?"

"Ben, I mean, Alex, or should I say Alejandra, there are rules. Guidelines. Time-honored laws. You're fully aware. You signed an agreement when you were recruited to be a Resident. Your type rarely receives an invitation."

"My type?"

"Please, Benito. Don't insult us both."

"Why now? After all this time?"

"The Residents believe you've been punished enough. And nothing too harmful occurred that day of the explosion. You weren't to blame. Were you?"

"Wasn't I?"

"The bomb in the Grand Library. We know you didn't set it. And the damage was minimal at best."

"Minimal? Really?"

He tilts forward, collapsing the space between us and puts his hand on my knee. "Minimal." He repeats.

"I don't think the damage was minimal. Not at all. In fact, I think you and the Residents realize how easy it is for the Rebels to infiltrate your beloved Grand Library."

"Ah, Ben . . . I'm your friend, remember? I want to help you. You can get out of here. Just say the words."

"Let me think."

He reclines on the lavish chair and grins. He thinks he's won me over.

"What are the words? The Rebel fighting words? We will win the Woke Wars! Those words, Cicero? Are those the words you want to hear?"

He bobs his head to the White Guard, who then grips my forearm, twisting it, and rams me against the door.

"I'm not going back, Cicero." My cheek is pressed to the steel exit. The guard pushes against my back.

"Ponder this, Benito. Things here will only worsen. And we need you at the Grand Library. Who else is going to document the Rebellion? You as an insider are invaluable. And you'll be rewarded. For assisting. You can lead us to their cells. You do know América escaped? Hasn't been found. We fear for her.

And your friends. They plan another insurrection. Surely you want to help save their lives."

I spit, and the blob lands on his white slacks.

"Ah, Benito, Benito . . . do you presume we weren't watching you and your Rebel friends? You're far more naïve than I estimated."

He stands, faces me and sets a hand on my shoulder in that tender custom that had consistently generated trust. I want to pummel his face, but decide I made my point.

"Tell the Counselor that Benito is ready for his interrogation," says Cicero. "And tell him not to go easy this session."

"My name is Alejandra."

TAMAYA

Tamaya's lineage went back more than thirty thousand years to the four corners of the continent. During those millennia, they had perfected hybrids of squash, beans, corn and potatoes, among other tubers, and thrived from their harvests. Their home of crisp, pure air and plateaus and marvelous mountain formations had been molded over six-hundred million years.

"No fucking Bering Straits for us," Tamaya's grandmother would declare to her grandchild, spilling stories of a time when extended kin grew together, traversing hills and streams, inhabiting caves and dwellings on cliffs. They honored bald eagles that guided them through travails of heat and cold.

"We are born here, like the trees and the boulders, and we age like the stars. You can touch them, Tamaya. Go ahead."

Tamaya, her grandmother and an aunt lay on a blanket, gazing up on a moonless night.

"Don't forget," her grandmother reminded Tamaya, "you are a warrior."

"Leave the girl alone," her auntie interrupted the lesson.

Each winter, their family camped inside a cave for weeks until they had hunted enough food to take back to their clan. Now, they had emerged from their cavernous shelter to gaze at the infinite universe. Her auntie, nestled beside Tamaya, handed her a four-inch blade with a smooth, flat grip. Tamaya sat up promptly, tested the sharp edges with a finger and pressed the tip to her palm.

"Careful," said her auntie.

"You sharpened it."

Her auntie bowed toward a lone piñon. "Let's see how sharp."

Tamaya stood erect, legs apart with left foot forward and right slightly back. She gauged the distance to the piñon. At least six feet. A full spin would hit her target. Gripping the flat handle, the sharp edge toward the ground, she took in a breath, exhaled and let loose, and the blade spun through air. It pierced the bark in a solid thud. She went to the tree, seized the steel, retraced her steps and threw the knife again. This time, no spin. This time, she pitched harder, and the thud was louder.

Her grandmother nodded. Auntie grinned in the darkness.

For the rest of her life, Tamaya would hold them deep inside her, always her arbiters of time, her progenitors of love. When she faced loss, she would return to the same cave. Alone. She'd sit and dream, hear their voices, plan to enact their wishes. There in a corner, propped against a boulder in the cave, she looked at herself in an obsidian mirror, contemplating who and what she'd become. She would step inside the opaque glass, disappear to reappear.

～∽～∽～

Out from some cryptic underworld she came. Tamaya entered the café as if time had not passed, as if weeks had not elapsed. She was dressed in tan camouflaged, military fatigues with the shirt unbuttoned at the top.

"I've been looking for you," she said.

"No. You haven't," I replied.

"Suit yourself." Tamaya then shouted to Fidel, "*Amigo*, bring me a tequila."

He rolled his eyes impatient with her absurd request and brought over an indigo bottle with a gold label embossed with the word "*Agua*." Tequila had not been outlawed, it just wasn't available anymore. Or maybe it was no longer produced. Desert flora had been infected by blight in the region of former Mexico and since then, their juices had dried up.

Tamaya snatched the bottle of upscale water and took a lengthy, deliberate, accentuated pull. She slammed the bottle down hard on the table and wiped her mouth with the back of her hand. I wondered what the display was about.

"How's life?" she asked.

"How's life? That's your question after weeks of hiding?" I asked.

"Hiding? Who's hiding? You could've come to see me anytime. Fidel, why didn't you tell Alejandra where to find me?"

Fidel rolled his eyes again and proceeded to stir a ten-gallon pot of something that smelled delicious. He must have envisioned an army that day.

"Why didn't you come see me?" she asked.

"Why didn't you come see me?" I answered.

"Simple. I don't know where you live."

"There you have it."

"There I have what?"

"I don't know where you live either."

I waited for her response, but she only glared across the table at me. Her silence made me uncomfortable.

"I didn't know you were back," I said.

"Of course, I'm back. We have work to do. How many times do I have to tell you, Alejandra?"

"Tell me? Tell me what?"

Tamaya sloped forward, resting her breasts on the table. She smelled of citrus. After a long, thirty seconds of a staring match, she crossed her arms.

I didn't speak and she didn't move.

"You're no Rebel," I said.

"Oh?"

"You're playing at revolution, Tamaya. You and your Rebel friends. You use these kids."

She blinked. Her lips tightened, and then she blew out a long, soft breath.

"You act like revolutionaries, but as far as I can see, you walk around pretending. You're no different from me."

Her face froze. Finally, she nodded and smiled, her grin widening her cheeks.

My face must have flushed because I suddenly realized how angry I was. "You've asked me to give up so much. And for what?" I heard my voice grow louder. "What are you giving up? What have you given up?"

"Your questions are all wrong, Alex."

"Not for me."

I glared, unwilling to relent.

"A true revolutionary act, Alex, can you name one?"

Tamaya chuckled and I was convinced she only laughed to annoy me more.

"Your mother was right," she said.

"My mother?"

"Your mother."

"My mothers are gone. They're both gone. They died years ago."

"Sure. Technically, they're gone."

Tamaya tossed a piece of paper onto the middle of the table. It had been ripped from a page in a book with tiny print. In the margins someone had scrawled numbers and a name.

"Meet me tonight. This address. And don't be late."

She rose from her chair and kicked its legs under the table.

"And by the way," I howled, "you're no revolutionary, either!"

Without turning, she yelled, "An authentic life, Ben. Consider that."

And she was gone.

I snatched the tattered fragment she'd left on the table and read the address.

"Fidel," I called out.

"Yes, my friend."

"Do you know this place?"

He came to the table and grasped the torn scrap, staining it with tomato sauce. Fidel had long thin fingers, the kind that play a piano or a classical guitar, but as far as I knew, Fidel was a cook and a driver, not a musician.

"5252 Celestial Drive," he said.

With index finger and thumb, he pinched the paper and poked it with his right index finger. He furrowed his brow and narrowed his eyes, lowering his head to render a double chin.

"Ah, yes. I know the address, yes." He hesitated and shook his head. I could see he was trying to hide the excitement on his face. His eyes widened.

"You, Alejandra, will not survive in such a place. You cannot go alone." He walked back to his open kitchen behind the granite counter.

"Fidel, why the secrecy? What is this place?"

"Not a place for the sweet, innocent Alejandra."

He mumbled to himself while chopping an onion.

"You will not survive the evening. Thieves, hooligans and gangsters frequent that tavern. You will not survive."

"Come with me," I said, surprising myself.

"Go with you? Why me?"

"I thought you were my friend, Fidel."

"A cook who feeds you daily and plays a game of checkers with you is not really a friend, is he? Let me ask you this. How many children do I have, Dr. Espinoza?"

He had me there.

"Do I live here? In the café? Why did I fly you to Tamaya and our undisclosed sanctuary? Do you have answers to any of these questions? No, you do not."

As he lectured, I sank lower in my chair, embarrassed and regretful. My usual sin of self-absorption. Today was the first day I began to consider who Fidel was and where he came from.

"What time?" he asked.

"What time?" I repeated.

"I close the café at midnight every night. I'll ask my husband to close for me."

"Thank you." And I had nothing more to say, although I was more than grateful.

"Don't thank me. You might not be so appreciative once we're inside that outlaw saloon."

Saloon? Fidel often mimicked characters from the nineteenth century, when cattle rustlers roamed the Wild West. I relished his tales of yore recast with antiquated vocabulary that no one spoke anymore. Not that he cared. He was not one to bother with others' opinions. Yet in all those tales, he never spoke of himself or his family. Instead, his stories were from slick magazines and trash novels he preserved in his own library, which consisted of books piled from the floor to the ceiling in the back room of the café. He encouraged customers to browse the collection, and I had perused the stacks, finding nothing of interest, yet still curious, hoping to stumble across a gem.

SAGUAROS

Because it was too early to go to the tavern at 5252 Celestial Drive, I walked back to my desolate apartment near the Grand Library and attempted to concentrate on a clumsy paragraph I'd written. But my thoughts were on Tamaya and the impending evening. What was the big mystery? Were Tamaya and Fidel in cahoots? Now, there's a word. Cahoots. Conspiring or colluding together to accomplish some unknown thing to outsiders. Isn't that what it meant? And I was the poor fool who was the outsider, not knowing once again, what the Rebels planned. It was unclear to me what Fidel's role was in this venture. He never claimed to be a Rebel, and yet he ran with the wolves, so to speak, who were obviously Rebels. During our games of checkers, he never spoke about his relationship to the insurgents who frequented his café. He was wrong about one thing, though. I may have never questioned his home life, but I had asked about his involvement in the rebellion. Each time, his response was the same: "That, my friend, is a mystery even to me." And that was that. He remained tight-lipped, maybe to protect me, maybe to keep me guessing.

My desk was beneath a narrow window that gave me a clear view of the empty streets below. No one walked alone at night for fear of being accosted either by the White Guard or by thugs who had no purpose other than to inflict havoc. And the White

Guard allowed the thugs to do as they pleased at night, never apprehending them, encouraging them to stage their marches with thousands, brandishing rifles and burning crosses. They were the threat that kept people at home at night and even for days at a time. The streets remained vacant from fear of being attacked or murdered by the Impresario's militia. None of the lawbreakers would be punished or brought to justice for their violence. They were the law.

Beside the window, I had a photograph I'd taken with my mothers when I was young. Most summers we traveled through the countryside together. One year, we drove to the desert, the legendary one with saguaros that stood thirty to fifty feet tall and were plentiful in the Sonoran desert. It had become my favorite destination because I relished the dry, desert heat. The giant saguaros were anywhere from one-hundred-and-fifty to two-hundred-years old, and I imagined them as the sentinels of the desert that witnessed families and friends assisting each other, living in unity. I decided they settled disagreements easily by playing a game with handmade leather balls made from deerskin. The winners would gain favor, and all would celebrate without any thought of reprisal against the group who'd lost. There was no retaliation, no revenge, no payback against the victors or the losers. Harmony reigned. My mothers, who idealized the past, told me such stories, and I grew fond of visualizing warriors tossing leather balls on sunny days. In any case, the wall exhibited my photograph of hundreds of saguaros with bright white blossoms dispersed on a hill. The sky was darkly indigo because I had managed to capture the stealthy blooms at night. This unique image of the desert filled my heart and captivated me in ways nothing before or after had.

Once, someone I brought back to my apartment stood in front of the photo and said, "Sentinels."

"What?" I asked.

"The sentinels never sleep," she said. "Is it true they only bloom at night?"

"Their flowers open at night. And most close the next day. There's a brief overlap," I said.

Her perfect dark-brown flesh glistened from the crescent moon shining through the window. Turning to me, she asked, "But some stay open for all to see? In the light of day?"

I replied, "Yes, some do."

AURELIO (RUSTY)

I showered and dressed in my uniform of tan khakis, white button-down shirt and brown blazer with standard elbow patches. I tightened the leather belt to hold up the loose pants. The body-hugging khakis had loosened with my body's transformation, and I noted how comfortable I felt. At the door of my apartment, I slipped on my tan shoes and knotted the laces. My feet had not reduced in size, of that I was relieved. I reveled in their length and width for no other reason than that I liked them. With a parting glance in the mirror, I pondered one thing: I didn't want to shift into Ben again.

Night had fallen, and the full moon shimmered blood-red. I had no need to use a flashlight tonight on my route to the café. Besides, light would draw attention that I didn't need. I entered the customary back entrance and met Fidel's glance as he spoke with a man who resembled him.

"Alejandra, we were just discussing you," said Fidel. "Come, please, meet my husband, Aurelio."

"Call me Rusty," said Aurelio.

He held out his hand to shake mine, or I thought he wanted me to shake it. With a sharp blade, he poked and sliced into my index finger.

"Ouch!"

I drew my finger to my mouth, but he pulled my hand, pinched the finger and rubbed the oozing blood on a pink cotton handkerchief. I yanked my hand away and sucked on my finger to soothe the sting from the cut.

"Don't worry, my friend," said Fidel, "it's a slight puncture. You'll heal quickly."

Aurelio, or Rusty, folded the handkerchief and tucked it inside the pocket of his olive bomber jacket. I noted his handsome features. He was stocky with muscular, dark-brown arms and a plump belly. Obviously, he enjoyed Fidel's cooking as much as I did.

"Aurelio is a *brujo*, an old school witcher . . . the kind your *abuelas* frequented."

"What would you know about my grandmothers, Fidel?" I asked.

"An absurd question, Alejandra."

"I thought *brujos* were a thing of the past," I said, obviously insulting Aurelio without intending to. Well, maybe I did want to upset him. The man had just cut my finger and drawn blood without my consent.

"What do you intend to do with my blood sample?"

He patted his bomber jacket, and a poof of air burst out from his inside pocket. "This?" he said. "It's my insurance."

"Insurance for what?"

"Come, we must go before it gets too late," Fidel said, grabbing my elbow and leading me out the back door of his café.

"Fidel? What was that about?" I wasn't about to let him off the hook. "What did he mean, "insurance"? Am I going to die?"

"You've already died and are reborn. Come, jump in my wagon."

I wanted to pursue my inquiry but realized he would only change the topic or respond with more questions. His wagon was an old jalopy, by twenty-first-century standards, even though it was electric, with faux wooden panels below each of the four doors, resembling a tree in route to somewhere or something. Inside, ripped leather seats with sharp rusted springs poked out, forcing one to push the wires aside or get scratched.

I attempted to sit closer to the passenger door to avoid the rusty coils. The door itself had remnants of a wooden panel now ripped out to display the door's inner frame. I pushed down the button that locked it, not because I feared someone would open it, but because I thought it might fly open as Fidel zoomed around bends and curves. I gripped the door handle.

"Fidel, why the rush?"

"Rush? Ah . . . my high speed is reckless? I see. This is the way I drive when there's no one on the road. You have nothing to fear."

"No one is ever on the road, Fidel."

"Oh, a few of these electric machines still run."

As he zipped down streets, I tossed around in the front seat and, instead of panicking, I sat back and tried to convince myself we were not about to ram into the next streetlamp. Fidel swept around more curves, and I suspected we were traveling in circles, until I realized we were in a maze. This section of the city was unfamiliar to me, and without Fidel, I wouldn't have discovered the obscure address at the end of a circular maze. I wondered if the elusive cook was merely trying to confuse me by traversing corners so recklessly that I couldn't focus on the route. Without warning, he slammed on the breaks, and my head tossed forward and back. His right, thick arm stretched out across my torso as if to protect me from hitting the windshield. In fact, his beefy limb probably had protected me.

"We're here," he announced.

"Here?"

"Yes, here."

"But there's nothing here."

Celestial Drive

A wooden gate and fence at the end of a paved road obstructed any further passage. Shades of orange, turquoise, emerald green and rose pink layered the wooden fence with shavings of colors sprinkled on the grass. There was a whimsical quality to the scene.

Fidel jumped out, unlocked the gate, bounced back into the jalopy and drove through a gate to a meadow at the edge of a forest.

"Fidel, what is this place? There's no address anywhere."

"Have some faith, Alejandra."

Again, he stopped the car and hopped out. He walked around to open my door, not because he performed a gallant gesture from last century but because the door was wired shut and had to be unfastened from the outside. I trembled, despite the evening's warmth—my nerves were shot. I got out and trailed my driver down a path until we reached a palo verde. On that tree, I saw the address, 5252 Celestial Drive, scratched illegibly in broad, huge letters and numbers. The address was suspended from a heart-shaped wooden panel that had been nailed to the tree's slim trunk. Perplexed, I paused to examine the scene.

"Come, my friend. They're waiting."

"Waiting? Who's waiting?"

"The gang's all here," he quoted an old Hollywood film, apparently pleased with himself for making the reference.

"Gang? What gang, Fidel? I don't know any gangs."

"Ah . . . why be so literal?"

He escorted me through an iron gate that squeaked as he pushed it open, and I shut it behind us. A winding path stretched to yet another gate and, on closer inspection, I detected ornate woodcarvings of moths on double doors as high as fifteen feet, perhaps more. The doors opened slowly, like a hesitant invitation into a narrow, dim entryway. I thought, of course, here's the archetypal long, dark narrow hallway leading to a crypt. I wasn't wrong. The hallway coiled in circles like another maze, which filled me with paranoia as I became disoriented, sure there would be no way out. My claustrophobia subsided when we entered a crowded ballroom throbbing with loud music and enraptured dancers. There was a disco globe floating above its center but attached to nothing, because the ceiling opened to the sky. Pristine air that smelled of oranges wafted in from above us. When I looked down, I couldn't see the floor or my shoes, because the surface was swathed in a steamy fog that resembled clouds of assorted colors. The earsplitting music, which sounded like disco from the late twentieth century, inundated the room from speakers mounted high on the walls. I looked around the crowd of dancers for Tamaya, who had not warned me that I would be attending a dance party like the ones from last century. My mothers had met in a place like this and often spoke of their nightclub days with such nostalgia that it seemed they had lived in the 1970s, but of course they hadn't.

"Fidel!" I screamed over the loud, pulsating music, despite being a few inches from his face.

He curled his eyebrows in acknowledgment while in an earnest conversation with a man who towered above Fidel. The giant wore jeans with leather chaps and a leather vest, which exposed a silky, hairless chest with tattoos. I could not make out the shape of his tattoos, but I didn't care because I had questions for Fidel, who raised both hairy eyebrows again.

The room teemed with euphoric Descendants. Beauties bopped ecstatically with each other in pairs, in trios and in big clusters. I guessed they were taking the drug of the year, something called "castle in the sky," which had not been outlawed despite warnings that too much of the drug caused permanent psychological damage. The dancers bounced around, and I have to admit that their leaps and twirls made me happy. They reminded me of the Descendants in the sanctuary who had swayed and hopped in unison or individually before it was blown up by the invaders. Here in this peculiar hide-away far from the city, Descendants had free-will and transformed with ease, shifting as they pleased.

"Come," said Fidel.

I didn't hear him, but I could decipher the words he mouthed.

He grabbed my elbow and pushed me in front of him and behind his tall, husky leather-clad friend. Sandwiched between them, I must have looked slight, since both towered above me, but in my mind, I was big. As Ben, I was average height, and as Alejandra, I wasn't as tall, but I considered myself grander than Ben. I had a newfound confidence. Sometimes.

We maneuvered through the crowd and bumped our way through another hallway leading to chambers with no doors. Inside each room, more blissful Descendant shifters danced to music designated for that zone. We passed a room with Caribbean sounds in which a black, silky-skinned woman sang on a stamp-sized stage while twirling her sequined gown. As we shuffled past another sector, we heard the jazz of a measured, sultry electric guitar resounding from the speakers. Round tables that seated three or four people crowded the room. Another chamber had raucous rock and roll in one corner, heavy metal and mosh pits in an additional corner, and quiet, grunge-depressed folx in another spot, although they didn't seem depressed. Their lyrics sounded optimistic if somewhat self-pitying, but not in an annoying, pompous way, more like a welcome melancholia that heals the heart. I paused, pondering self-reflective lyrics about death and depression, but the contrast of low bass notes further away floated closer, and in the distance I saw dusky brown teenagers circle the dance floor, floating up and down in a one-two rhythm. I was drawn to the blues room, which had blue painted walls and blue electric lights shimmering on the young soul folx playing electric guitars and singing in ways that stirred me. I wanted to sit and take it all in. An old Lead Belly song about the Scottsboro Boys from as far back as the 1930s and another tune by Sister Rosetta Tharpe gave me a faith I could not explain. What was it about the blues that healed? Like that John Lee Hooker song with Santana? Or songs like Chitlins and Carne. The fusion of cultures and sounds and food, it was all here on Celestial Drive. Rooms and spaces that roused you to become the best of who you wanted to be.

In these spaces, Descendants shifted with such ease and beauty that no one would doubt how they had grown accustomed to this style of transformation. We were outside the threat of the capital city, where the White Guard tamed every inch of our feelings. Not since I'd been in the sanctuary had I felt this infectious freedom. I began to realize that my own shifting was so much more than the transformation of a physical body. The shifting had everything to do with an overwhelming inner joy, experienced as if everything held hope, a hope that would lead us to pursue our freedom. Including the freedom to shift openly. Outwardly.

It was here I saw Burgundy Boy standing erect on a stage, crooning the poetry of yearning love songs, his purplish-crimson-tan skin glistening. He hopped down from the stage, seized my hand, and we swayed as he breathed in my ear. He threw back his head, laughed and began to morph. His body-mind mingled and fused into a kind of corporal duality until suddenly, there she stood: Tamaya.

"It's you!" I said.

"Surprised?"

"I am. I didn't know you could sing."

Tamaya smiled and waved at a young black shifter with exceptionally broad shoulders. He sauntered to the stage, leapt up and crooned one of those archaic *boleros* my mothers loved, the ones about broken hearts and longing and despair for a love that could never be, never would be "because you broke my heart, you fucker, so now get the fuck outa my house." Maybe not like that, but that was how I remembered the Mexican ballads as the broad-shouldered shifter sang.

"Damn song," I said.

"It's a classic."

"My mothers loved it."

"What happened to them?" she asked.

"Who?"

"Your mothers."

"Let's just say their love didn't last into eternity."

"You don't know that, Alejandra."

"I don't?"

"You don't."

"Maybe I don't," I responded.

"For all you know, the taste of each other's lips still lingers."

"You don't strike me as a romantic, Tamaya."

"Who said anything about romance?"

"'*Sabor a mí*' is about as romantic and fantastical as you can get."

"Romance and fantasy are romance and fantasy, Alex. They aren't love. You should know that, Dr. Espinoza."

"Maybe. Maybe not."

"Did you take one of those stupid pills handed out at the front door? Seriously."

"Seriously what?"

"When are you going to commit to something. Anything. Make a choice to be alive at least."

We glided so smoothly that I forgot we were dancing. I focused on her lips and reminisced about the last time I'd kissed her. It had been too long. Weeks. Days. Hours.

"You're so fatalistic this evening. *¿Qué te pasa?*"

"*¿Qué me pasa?* You're actually asking me that?"

"Actually, I am."

"What's this game you're playing?"

"Not a game."

She whirled as I held her fingers lightly, rendering an effortless spin, and faced me. The comfort with which we swayed unsettled me.

"Follow me," she said and gripped my hand tightly.

I obeyed, and we crawled through the congested room that had become more jammed since the broad-shouldered, black crooner had begun singing, '*Sabor a mí*.' The song, over a century old, sustained ridiculous notions of eternal love. What a bunch of bunk, I thought. We inched through the mass of varied dancing partners—kindred shifters and soul folx, all of whom floated in a space that aroused them to transmute into variations of gendered physiques. I scrutinized the subtle fluctuations executed just as Tamaya had morphed a few minutes earlier. I envied them. These expert soul folx not only embraced who they were, but they also adopted what they could do after years of practice. If you weren't paying attention, you wouldn't see the metamorphosis. And it wasn't so simple as seeing men become women and women become men. There was more to the transmutation than blending of genders and sexes. These soul folx not only negated inadequate notions of "men as men" and "women as women," but they also defied those impositions in these playful halls.

What had been considered "maleness" or masculinity posed prettily as muscle-bound, bearded beauties in flamboyant rainbow-colored skirts whirling as they danced across a slippery floor in five-inch red heels, while the so-called feminine bodies twirled and stomped in brown combat boots. Next, I spotted angelic faces in tight dresses with low-cut bodices accentuating plump or small breasts. So much called to be explained but would remain unexplained because there was nothing to make clear. How do you reconcile your own limited beliefs when something simple is what it is because it's always been what it was willing to become outside of the strict parameters that were once considered the sex and gender of the last century? I had buried that part of me from fear and lack of conviction, but I'd always been a shifter. Now, as I faced myself with others like me, I submitted to a mood of belonging. Tamaya had cleverly devised this scheme, but at the time, I was unaware of her intentions.

Dancers paused and greeted Tamaya, hugging her close and kissing both her cheeks, which she returned, delaying our exit. I didn't complain. I was reminded of family fiestas when *primos*, *primas*, *tíos*, *tías*, *abuelas*, *abuelos*, *compadres* and *comadres* would spend an additional hour exiting parties because everyone had to embrace in familial recognition. There was no slipping out the back at these family fiestas.

For a moment, I was happy. Tamaya shone in the light cast from above the roofless chamber. When I looked down, a thin strip of multicolored fog floated above our shoes and heightened the movement of shuffling legs. The mist was brightly lit, and I took the moment to inspect my environment because something was familiar to me, more familiar than the familial caresses and greetings. I couldn't understand any of it.

"I'll be back," said Tamaya.

I groaned.

A group of young female-type shifters surrounded her, and they babbled all at once to each other and to Tamaya.

"Where are you going?"

"Just wait for me here. I'll be back," she said.

Tamaya led the way for the group of five, and they disappeared though a brightly lit hallway.

I was annoyed. I turned to walk out of the room and marched in the opposite direction from Tamaya and her crew. A strong grip clutched my forearm and twisted me around.

"Dammit, Fidel," I said.

He loosened his grip but didn't let go. "You look like you're rushing off, my friend."

"I'm not."

"Good, because we aren't done here."

"You're full of secrets, aren't you, Fidel?"

"We have a mission, Dr. Espinoza."

"A mission?"

"Tamaya is returning soon with explicit instructions."

He pushed me onto a spindly chair. Fidel tossed on my lap a pamphlet with the word "*VOLUNTAD*" on the cover, embossed in gold. I opened the first page to a list of five decree-like commandments:

1. Lies, greed and envy breed hate.
2. Free your soul from hate.
3. Free yourself to love.

4. Be kind, be willing.
5. Imagine, if you will.

The succinct list, while ridiculously naïve, emitted an optimistic mandate. To imagine. Another future.

"What's this, Fidel?"

"Isn't it obvious? Our manifesto."

"It's kind of brief to be a real manifesto."

"Is it?"

I shrugged and read the list out loud. "Seems naïve to me." I scoffed.

"Our fledgling revolutionaries authored the list."

Fidel took the pamphlet from my hands and tucked it inside his back pocket. He shook his head. "You are not beyond hope, Alejandra."

"I don't pretend to be."

"You pretend. You want us all to believe that you remain the cynical Dr. Espinoza, don't you?"

"I am who I am, Fidel."

"You only pretend to be who you are not," he said.

The last statement fueled me, and I suspect he planned to rouse me. I slowed my breath and rose from the squeaky chair. I brushed my short tresses back with my palm, relishing the return of waves I'd had as young Ben, when girls smoothed my full head of hair and called me Emo-boy at the camp. I stood in front of Fidel, burrowed my eyebrows and glared at him.

Fidel chuckled. "My friend, you are changing right before my eyes."

I fidgeted. "Fidel, since when have you been interested in this so-called revolution?"

"I never said I wasn't. My role is different."

"And what is that?" I asked.

"Many say I'm a guardian."

"A guardian? Like an angel?"

"Perhaps."

I was about to ask more questions about his role, which I thought was really cook and courier, but Fidel ignored me and turned to speak to a huddle of friends. They were dressed in military fatigues like the ones worn by Tamaya earlier that day. Tamaya stood among the group and gave detailed instructions to the crew of kindred shifters, also in brown camouflage, baggy pants held up with thick cloth belts and silver buckles. One by one they disappeared from the congested room after having listened carefully to Tamaya's directives. When all were gone, she turned to me.

CAVES, MIRRORS, TIMELINES

"It's time, Alejandra. Come," she said.

"Time? Time for what?"

She ushered me down the bright corridor she had disappeared into earlier in the evening. When we reached a set of double doors, she swung them open and steered me inside the mouth of a cave that stretched into an expanse so deep I couldn't see where it led. Lodged on the walls were mirrors, and I met myself reflected ten times over until hundreds of faces materialized, shuffling in and out of each other into multiple distinctive bodies. They became clearer, floating toward me.

"It's a timeline, Alejandra."

"Timelines are imaginary," I responded.

"Of course, they are. That's why you can see into multiple timelines in the mirrors. The past, the future, all melded with the present."

"That makes no sense."

I regretted the statement when Tamaya talked to someone inside the mirror. I recognized the dialect as one of many spoken by our ancestors. It was a language our predecessors had preserved and passed on to younger generations, but few communicated in the idiom anymore, because if you were heard articulating the forbidden, you could be rounded up, questioned, perhaps detained permanently. Dialect crossers, as they were called, were not permitted to speak their language. You had to trust that the person you talked to would not report you to the White Guard. I've neglected to say that my mother, the one who was also a Descendant, had passed on her own dialect to me.

"Time folds in on itself. It's not linear. You, of all erudite scholars, should know this."

"I'm listening," I said.

"It's a portal. Portals can only be seen inside the mirrors in special caves. The mirrors reflect those who are invisible outside the portals."

"Why here?"

"It's sacred. The ancestors visit these portable mirrors but only inside caves. We have to be quick about it because the glass chamber will disappear soon."

I paused to consider the logic that had no logic. "Disappear?"

"Not exactly disappear. The ancestors move on. Taking the portal elsewhere. Space and time are not static, Alex. A simple concept even for you."

Tamaya liked to mock my näive mind despite my ardent attempt to grasp what she referred to as basic quantum "non-realities."

"Things only appear to be what we want them to be," she reassured me. ". . . If you just stop and pay attention, Alex."

All I could do was listen, as I studied the portal that looked like a mirror I could step into. But I was afraid I'd never return.

"She's here, by the way," said Tamaya.

"Who?"

I looked at her as if she was insane. She seemed to know what I was thinking, but in typical Tamaya fashion, ignored my reasoned logic and stepped out of the mirrored chamber, leaving me alone to do who knows what. Then it happened. A face and body walked toward me. I only recognized her as one recognizes fiction, something that has never happened and yet is still a memory buried in one's psyche. I thought she wasn't real and that I had conjured her in this symbolic space with an imaginary timeline.

"It's me," she said.

"*¿Mamá?*"

My eyes watered. I clenched both fists tightly, digging nails into the plump flesh of my palms.

After she faded into the glass, hiding, she reappeared and announced, "Sacred rage. Use your sacred rage, Alejandra."

When she pointed to my bleeding hands, I quickly wiped them on my pants, and the blood dissolved. She smiled at me.

"You're here," I said.

"I'm here, Alejandra. Remember, what we taught you. Descendants are drawn to each other like ancient souls pulled together for lifetimes. Encoded with purpose. A sacred rage."

She vanished, and I heard shrill, heartrending cries. My tears flowed like streams on to a prairie of dry desert cactus eager to be replenished. Sacred rage? I heard myself wailing. I didn't know if I wailed as the child Benito, the oblivious Dr. Ben Espinoza, or the raw rebel Alejandra. In that darkness, I howled until my rational mind paused on the word, "lachrymose" . . . a word fitting for the moment. Here was Ben reasoning, seeking logic where there was none. A desert prairie, once dry and empty, now lachrymose, I ruminated. There, I felt better.

GAMES

"Papi," you address me.

"*¿Qué m'ija?*"

"Did you forget?"

"Forget?"

"You forgot parts of the story, didn't you?"

"I'm sorry, Yareli. I guess I did."

You see the bruises on my face, the blood caked on my nose and forehead. I had just returned from the interrogation room with a pummeled face. A pink-cheeked Counselor had harangued me, as instructed by Resident Cicero. I had rearranged a handful of details, knowing he'd report back to Cicero. The Counselor followed the script of my testimony and, when he found discrepancies in the story, his pudgy fingers scrawled notes on a tablet with a digital pen. He looked up from his round, gold, wire-framed glasses, examining my face, and nodded to the White Guard in the corner of the windowless room. The nod meant two things: the interrogation was over and the White Guard had permission to beat the day's culprit.

"Papi."

You pat my forehead and wipe the blood from my face. You don't cry. You're strong. Getting stronger. I'm proud of you but fear your fluency with cruelty will only serve to numb you.

"Should I start at the beginning?" I ask you.

"No."

You have begun to realize what my suspicious mind has already surmised—that the details of my story are inconsequential. The Counselors will do as they please, but I play along at your game because I don't want you to lose faith. I don't want you to stop believing in love and life and humanity despite this forsaken prison where we remain stunted and timid. Outside, we were in a persistent state of becoming, leaping into a void, willing to be different, willing to risk everything to love differently.

That night, the depraved White Guard Miller unbolts the children's cage, the cage with the cinnamon girl whose baby sister had died. We dread the guard and his ritual. He singles out a child, retrieves them and we never see the child again. Tonight, Miller turns off the lights and in stark darkness, we hear small feet scramble to a corner. Children press tightly into a ball, wishing their globe of human flesh will protect them. He swings the wire door open, goading the children to escape, but it's only a game—to run for their lives. There is nowhere to run. Instead, they bury their tiny heads into each other's warmth, terrified of what will come next. He advances slowly, brushes his fingers across their heads, halts and drags a child from the circle. He yanks brutally and dislocates a tiny shoulder. The chosen child screams and the others cry.

"Papi, he's doing it again," you say.

I nod and squeeze you closer, grateful that your thirteen years protect you from the children's cage. Your body tenses as you tighten your muscles. I start to rise from the floor, ready to shriek at Miller for his savage game, but you tug me back down.

"Papi, please don't."

I pause, nestle you closer. I can't let go.

MILITANTS

Tamaya returned and escorted me to her crew of militants in brown T-shirts. It was then I noticed an emblem on the upper left corner of the cotton shirts. A circle with a pyramid inside the circle, and each line that shaped the pyramid had print. I had to inch in closer to read it. The closer I examined it, the more I saw an image made of words. I couldn't decipher the words. I would have needed a microscope, but what I did see was the shape of a winged creature that resembled a moth. A gray-brown moth with iridescent wings in flight. What a strange emblem, I thought. Brown moths.

A teenage girl placed her hand over the emblem on her T-shirt. It was only then I recognized Lucy as one of the militant crew.

"What are you doing here?" I asked.

"Same thing you are," she said, smirking, then looked away. "Everybody ready?"

"Ready, Chief!" a group of Descendant teenagers, all kindred shifters, shouted.

They were about ten or more shoving me along and I had no choice but to move with them.

"Where's Tamaya?" I asked.

"On a mission."

"Mission?"

"You'll see."

But it wasn't Lucy speaking. I listened for the voice in the crowd as the group propelled me forward. We headed down the path from which Fidel and I had arrived. As soon as we left behind the odd, roofless mansion, the young person who had spoken before stood in front of me.

"Get in." It was Z, who loomed over me.

Z pointed to a military helicopter that I recognized from photographs of the Vietnam War in the 1960s. It was one of those Sea Stallions used for heavy lifting and rescue missions with plenty of seats if extra cargo wasn't taking up space. Who and what was outfitting this rebellion? I jumped into the vehicle, landed on a ripped bucket seat and wrapped a rusted harness around my arms. I couldn't get the thing to click shut, which worried me. Teen shifters sat down in the seats that lined each side of the cabin and adjusted their harness seat belts. Since mine was faulty, I held it snugly against my chest and said a prayer to myself. I looked up and down the rows to empty spots and realized the cabin was larger than I had thought.

"Everybody in?" asked América.

She was propped in the pilot's seat, and I sat close by.

"What are you doing here?" I asked.

"I'm your pilot. Isn't it obvious?"

"Is this thing safe?" I asked. "It doesn't feel safe."

"Why wouldn't it be?"

I held up the seatbelt's loose strap to show her. América stood up, bent over me and pulled gently, allowing the spool to retract, then slipped the tongue into the buckle. The secure click satisfied me. She smiled and returned to the cockpit.

"Are you sure you can fly this thing?" I asked.

She ignored me and busied herself with dials and buttons that meant nothing to me.

"And the gas? I read that these old Sea Stallions burn a lot of fuel."

She turned her head to look at me. "We steal the fuel. Just like we stole the helicopter, Alex. What do you think? That we have benefactors?"

"Don't you?"

América shook her head and pulled on levers for flight. The noise from the propellers unsettled me.

"Where are we going?" I asked.

"Don't you know?"

"I do not."

"Tamaya didn't tell you?"

"She did not."

"You'll know soon enough."

All I knew was that I was in a military machine with América and her crew of teenage shifters and Lucy was buckled in beside me.

I leaned into her shoulder and asked, "Lucy, why won't anyone tell me where we're going?"

"Tamaya gave us strict instructions," she said.

"What am I, a child?"

"It's the rescue mission you asked for."

I heard América shout, and I saw Lucy smile. I suspected I was the butt of their joke.

I yelled to address the Rebel sitting across from us. "What's your name?"

"Her name is Tanda," said Lucy. "She doesn't say much."

"I'm not asking her to say much."

"Just telling you . . . She's one of the shy ones. But she gets things done."

"Gets things done? Like?"

"Like things that need to get done."

I glanced out of the window and saw moths flying beside us. I couldn't understand how the throng sustained pace with the vehicle.

"You've never seen that many, have you?" asked Lucy.

"Not like this. Where do they come from?"

"Souls," she said.

"Souls?"

"Yeah, souls that want to help us. Really, they're already dead. In life, they had fought the regime. Now . . ."

She spun away from me. Something told me not to pursue the topic with Lucy, who easily fell into moods, and I didn't want to be the cause of any mood, certainly not now when we were on our way to who knows where. The cadre of young Rebels I accompanied held each other's hands firmly, perhaps for reassurance, perhaps to reaffirm their camaraderie. Most of the time, I was flooded with guilt for not having fought hard enough for this generation. What they inherited was unfair at best. An autocratic Global Order, a kleptocracy. And then, I wondered, what do they believe in? Is another future possible? Are they making their way to something new? But what did these adolescents know? They were both naïve and skeptical. Somehow within their own rotten existence they held faith. Maybe rebellion does nurture optimism. What they didn't know is that nothing changes, even when we strive for change, even when we battle with every nerve ending, with every last ounce of will. We battle evil, and there are few changes. Evil prevails. Here I was again, being tiresome as the predictable old Dr. Benito Espinoza.

"You don't talk like him anymore," Lucy said.

"What?"

"Tamaya says you don't talk like him anymore."

"Like who?"

"Like *who*?" she responded, incredulous, and twisted around toward Z, who sat beside her.

I knew who she meant but I wanted to hear her say it. "When did she say that?" I asked. I tapped Lucy on the shoulder. "When did Tamaya say that about me?"

She ignored me, and I returned to my window, anticipating a glimpse of the terrain but all I saw was thick fog on the horizon. Lucy cuddled up next to Z and whispered something. They giggled as Z's fingers twirled her friend's strands of hair. Lucy pressed in tighter, their heads touching softly. More giggles. I looked out the window again. When was the last time I allowed intimacy like that? An intimate friendship with someone you love. I couldn't remember. Any reminder of the past only depressed me. I didn't like who I had been, I refused to acknowledge who I had become and I existed in relentless fear of becoming all I was required to be. Who could possibly love someone like me?

Then, as if inspired by the moment, the Rebel kindred shifters began to sing. The tune was recognizable, and when they reached the chorus, I remembered it was one of those spirited revolutionary songs that had been banned long before they were born. I wondered how they knew it so well.

Lucy and Z led everyone in the song that had complex, drawn-out lyrics. The curious thing is that, like the title of the song, "*Volver a los 17*" (To Return to Age 17), none of them could ponder being seventeen again. Everyone knew the lyrics despite the song having been banned. Too many times it had roused the masses into rebellion. Too many times people had been massacred, and yet the Rebels continued to sing it and to teach it and to live by the promises it made, like something holy. The message was love, after all. And wasn't that what the Rebels stood for? Love of life, love of transformation, love of shifting—all that had been stifled from the human spirit.

The melancholic song depressed me. Maybe that was the point. To sink into such acute despair that I didn't care if I lived or died. Who would care? Who would miss me? Certainly not the Residents. As Alejandra, I didn't dare return to the Grand Library again. I feared the repercussions. The Residents would surely warn the authorities if I attempted to return. If Tamaya had wanted to sever me from my comforts at the Grand Library, she had succeeded.

Unexpectedly, the helicopter descended, and we landed on empty field.

"*¡Vámonos! ¡A liberar a los prisioneros!*" América shouted.

"What is she talking about?" I asked Lucy.

"Let's go," said Lucy.

MAD

We scooted out onto the grass. Red flags on each side of a paved road made a pathway. América walked to the front, and I stepped aside, counting twelve young shifters as they passed me. Because I wasn't sure of our destination, I stayed far back enough to run if I had to. Was I a coward? I thought we had already established that, but as I flanked the rear of the army, I regarded my purpose. I may have even believed myself a rebel with a real cause, whatever that might have been. Lucy turned around and beamed at me, perhaps pleased that I flanked the periphery of our private army.

"What?" I asked.

Lucy hopped a step to catch up to Z. We continued down the path marked by the red flags. There were dozens indicating the winding route. I wanted to stop and read the insignia on the flags, which looked like three letters in white: MAD. Of course.

MAD was the acronym used at the beginning of the twenty-first century when prisons were established to cage Descendants. The letters stood for "Massacre All Descendants," and the adage was touted by extremist ASSES and the White Guard acting on behalf of the Impresario. They were convinced that once they purged every last Descendant, their world would be perfect. They would seize, occupy and settle every inch of land that was never theirs.

América raised her right arm and pointed forward in a sweeping gesture. The group rushed forward, encircling her. She tipped her head and signaled with her chin toward a door on the far right, then singled out seven of the kindred shifters, who gathered in their own circle and disclosed what must have been a plan to proceed. I saw the group of seven disappear behind a ten to twelve-foot metal door that opened after they plugged numbers into hand-held computers. América turned toward me, and I marched to her side, not daring to defy her orders. Lucy and Z also obeyed and paused beside me. Three others gathered behind to protect us. Z punched numbers into a hand-held computer and a white wall opened to a garden. There were red and purple roses throughout the courtyard.

"Where are we?" I asked.

No one answered. Lucy motioned with her fingers, sliding them across her lips as if zipping her mouth closed. Z's eyes widened, and her head tilted toward a red door. The quiet girl named Tanda opened the door and tiptoed into an unlit room. I kept still in the middle of the garden, gazing up to the sky, which was not a sky at all but instead a dome painted with stars that glowed. I stared mesmerized by the big and little dippers, by Orion, by the warriors and bears and scorpions that filled the sky. The constellations shifted across the dome steadily, and I became as entranced as I had been as a child. I looked around and realized my comrades had disappeared. I was alone in the garden, when out of nowhere, he appeared. The Impresario.

"Well, well, well, if it isn't the great Benjamin Espinoza. I've been waiting for you and your trash."

I was perplexed, not only because he knew me by name, even if he got it wrong, but also because he seemed aware that the Rebels would be arriving at his mansion or whatever it was.

"What is this place?" I asked.

His tiny hand swept the air in front of him, and he said, "This? My retreat. For me and my friends. We need a place to blow off steam. Running the world isn't easy. And all you woke losers just won't stop, will you?"

The garden brightened when he touched a button against a green wall, and the wall split open.

"Come on," he said. "I wanna show you something."

I wasn't sure why I followed, but I did, and we walked through the divider to another area with multiple screens hanging on another green wall. On the monitors, the Rebels sped through hallways, opening doors to rooms with young girls and a few boys. The rooms brought to mind bedrooms from the last century decorated with Disney princesses, silk curtains and canopy beds. Pink dressers lined the walls, and on top were bowls brimming with foil-wrapped chocolates and cookies. The Rebels pulled the children from the rooms and escorted them through a hallway leading back to the main entrance. I saw Z stop and empty bowls of sweets into cargo pants, and Z's pockets drooped from the stash. The rescue was happening, and yet the Impresario wasn't paying attention. Instead, he poured bourbon into a crystal snifter and sipped it. He didn't offer me a drink, and I wondered if I would have accepted. Nervously, I watched the Rebels, anticipating the Impresario's next move. Surely, his White Guard would retaliate soon. I had no way of warning América or Lucy or Z.

"Oh, don't worry about that." He pointed at the monitors. "Plenty more where they came from," he said.

The Impresario reclined on a high back velvet throne with ornate wood carvings of a lion's head. "Come sit," he said.

I gaped at the displays of children and Rebels scurrying through narrow hallways with countless doors to more rooms in this palatial prison.

"Would you like a drink, Ben?" He held up his crystal snifter. "I mean, Alex, right? You go by Alex now? First, you're a shifter, then you're not a shifter, and now here you are standing in front of me looking like that. Come to think if it, I don't think I want to share my premium cognac with her."

His beady blue eyes scanned my body and he chuckled.

"You're a much better-looking man, Ben. If I was you . . ." his voice trailed off.

The smirk on his orange face and fake blue eyes made me want to punch him.

"Oh, don't be so serious, Ben. I mean, Alex. Damn, it is hard keeping up with you shifters and your names and what you want to be called. Can't you be normal like the rest of us?"

"This is normal?" I asked. "Keeping children imprisoned for you and your disgusting habits?"

"You're judging me? Really? You've got a lot of nerve. I mean, look at you. You're not even pretty. Hell, I wouldn't touch you with a ten-foot pole."

"They're children," I said, knowing he'd have his selfish rationale.

"I take care of these children. I feed them, clothe them. And look at their dorms. They're living in paradise. All the chocolates any kid could want."

He pointed at the screen to the stuffed, plush bears and lions strewn on canopy beds. "And toys! We give them toys!"

The Impresario crossed his legs and smoothed the pant leg with his palm.

"You want them out there? Homeless? Scrounging for rat food? They're safe here. Fully fed."

"You're lying," I said.

He smirked again and swallowed cognac from his snifter. He switched on another monitor and recognizable faces from the Grand Library materialized.

"Your buddies," he said. "You're just like them, aren't you, Ben?"

The Residents convened at a table teeming with delicacies. Cakes, breads, stews, puddings, cheeses, strawberries and grapes were spread across the rectangular, antique table. An ample roasted pig with an apple in its jaw decorated the table's center, and dozens of empty wine bottles lined a wall. More than twenty Residents guzzled red wine and gnawed gleefully on the roast pork, cackling and shouting epithets like endearments. I spotted Phillip and his cohort, which was predictable, but I was disheartened to see Cicero at the head of the table, laughing. It was unnerving to witness. I had been wrong about so much. And now, here in front of me all I may have mistrusted or denied was in front of me, tempting me to take up arms against these greedy, corrupt imbeciles. And I'd been one of them. But had I?

The Impresario's beady eyes squinted at me. I said and did nothing. I deliberately held back any reaction.

He punched a remote device over and over, targeting a screen that flickered with fuzzy images.

"Damn this fucking thing!"

He shouted and hurled the remote against the wall, shattered plastic pieces flew across the room. Then he pitched his snifter and broken chards flew everywhere, brown liquid streamed down the gold wallpaper. I reflexively raised my hand to where a piece of glass had grazed my cheek. The Impresario bellowed until two White Guards scurried in from another entrance.

"Everything all right?" asked the tall one.

"No, everything is not all right. Look at those screens! We're being invaded, and what are you morons doing?"

"Sir, you told us to stand back and stand down."

"Yeah, yeah, yeah."

He aimed at another monitor and ordered, "Fix that one. I want Ben to see the surgery room."

The tall guard swiftly punched a button. That's when I saw physicians with masks covering their mouths and wearing white, bloodied coats. Assistants hovered nearby, cradling trays with knives and scalpels. A child of no more than ten was unconscious on an operating slab. The view from the ceiling camera reminded me of the camps . . . with Marco. Blood spurted from the child's crotch, and an assistant sponged the area repeatedly as the physicians, two of them, severed sex organs.

"What the fuck?" I said to myself but loud enough for the Impresario to hear me.

"You know about these surgeries, don't you, Ben? This is how we fix the shifters. They'll never have to shift again. It's their freedom. They can be normal. Like the rest of us. Well, maybe not like you. But it's not too late. These doctors are the best in the world. They can fix you, too. And you can return to the Library with your buddies. They'll love you for it."

We're all trapped in this madman's whimsy, I thought. And those who follow the madman are just crazy. Prior to the camps, there were these special hospitals. If shifters, who had learned to live incognito, were caught, they would be sent to private hospitals for operations that sliced up their bodies, severing their sex organs. After the surgical trauma imprinted the body, shifting could no longer be done at the will of the contemplative mind. It was an amputation of will. But desire and the will to fulfill it can be powerful, and shifters were clever. Bodies held memories of a future already happening. For better or for worse, the practice had been outlawed and, instead, everyone was forced to register their sex at birth and carry a digitized file of birth records.

TRANSCENDERS

I heard footsteps and turned to see Lucy's quiet friend, Tanda, sneak inside the room. She walked straight up to the Impresario with open arms, and he enfolded her petite body to his chest.

"Well, well, looks like you brought me a present," he said.

Tanda winked at me as she slipped something into the Impresario's pant pocket. She quickly tore away from him, grabbed my hand and yanked me so fast that I didn't have a second to consider what was happening. I suspected what Tanda had done. An explosion ripped through the door and when we landed in the courtyard, fire began enveloping the roses. I spotted the Burgundy Boy crooner sprinting from another room and, as he slammed another door behind him, an explosion flung him next to me. He looked at me, promptly rose and took my hand. We ran fast along the footpath lined with blue and pink flags that had the emblem W5. I wasn't sure when the Rebels had removed all the MAD flags and replaced them, but they had been thorough. Not one red flag remained. The rescued shifters scrambled with us, and as they screamed, I couldn't decipher joy or tears in their cries, but it was probably a bit of both. Someone shoved me from behind into the helicopter. Already inside were the seven young shifters who initially had gone in the opposite direction.

The newly liberated girls and boys squeezed together. They gripped each other's hands and cried softly, burying heads in each other's shoulders. Dressed in white, their vibrant shades of black and brown skin glimmered in the cabin light.

A few seats away from me, a girl cowered, her cheek pressed against the Rebel sitting beside her. She whimpered, and my heart ached for this slight girl who had been imprisoned. I could only image the torture her small body had suffered. The Rebel put an arm around her and pulled the girl closer. She burst into tears and quieted again, repeating the same phrase, "*Me duele, todavía me duele tanto.*" The phrase, uttered like a prayer into the atmosphere, stung. She'd been hurt deeply, and that she still hurt made me angry.

I'd been so distracted, staring at the girl in the white lace dress that I hadn't noticed we were airborne with Z at the helm and Lucy also in the cockpit. I scanned the cabin and was relieved to see all twelve Rebels sitting in their assigned seats, securely fastened. Lining the walls in formerly empty seats were the rescued children. There must have been about twenty of them buckled tightly with a handful cross-legged on the cabin floor, clutching hands.

"Where's Señor Crooner?" I said out loud. "Where's Tamaya?"

No one answered. The Rebels remained quiet, and the liberated young shifters moaned gently. América sat beside me now that Lucy was co-pilot.

"América, did we just assassinate the Impresario?" I asked.

"That was the plan," she said.

"Why didn't you tell me? I thought we were on a rescue mission. Do you have any idea what you've done? We'll be crucified for this. They'll probably lynch us in some public square. Or line us up along a wall for a firing squad."

"Oh, stop worrying. Nobody suspects you. And no one knows you're with us."

"This whole crew knows! I know. The rescued kids know!"

"You should be celebrating. That's what we're going to do. Celebrate the moment with us, Alex. This gives us more time."

"Time? For what? To hide?"

"Nobody knows you're here, okay? Stop worrying."

"Time for what, América?"

"Time for more rescue missions, that's what. The ASSES will be so busy fighting each other to take power that they'll forget about us Rebels."

"Not for long."

"Long enough."

"And the White Guard? They'll look for us. You know that."

"So?"

"So? What do you mean, so?"

"Look around, Alex. We've saved more shifters. And we'll save even more in the next few weeks. Don't you care? And these shifters are special. They've had surgeries, most of them. That means they can transcend."

"Transcend? As in another consciousness or something? What does surgery have to do with that?"

"Sure, another consciousness. It's different. If you'd had the surgery, you'd know."

She stared at me, and I realized what she meant.

"You've had it. The surgery. At the camp," I said.

"I did. It freed me. And these kids, they understand that. We teach them to feel free. In a way, the surgeries facilitate a stronger, longer lasting transformation without having to worry or focus on whether the body will change when you're not ready for it to change. Instead, shifters learn to sustain their shift for as long as they want, whenever they want, however they want. So yes, it's another consciousness that gets ushered in after surgery.

And that's something the Ascendant-surveyors didn't plan on. Idiots. They thought they were amputating us, our will. They just made us tougher, more resilient, more rebellious. It's a whole new world happening, Alex. These young shifters, they get it. And the Impresario, he'll be replaced with another greedy dimwit, and we'll keep fighting, and we'll keep transforming and transcending when and how we want."

Aurelio (Rusty)

"Papi, you rescued the children," you say.

"Not me, *m'ija*."

"You were there. Weren't you?"

"Yes, I was there, *amor*."

Your mother calls you to join her and the Descendant women. You get up and skip toward her, but you stop when she tells you to bring your journal. I lift it from the floor and hand it to you. You smile.

I decide to take a break from the story. Aurelio, my most ardent eavesdropper, snores softly.

"I'm not asleep," he says. "Go on. And get to the end already. I don't have all day."

"You were snoring."

"I was breathing. That means I'm alive, not asleep, not dead either."

He swings his right leg as if to cross it over the absent left one and repositions his torso to pull a pink handkerchief from a back pocket. He holds it up to the florescent light to show me, then grasps it tightly in his fist. I rise to my feet and place a cushion beneath his head. It isn't really a cushion. The makeshift roll of rags doubles as a pillow and a suitcase packed with his few belongings.

"*Gracias.* Now, go on before I fall asleep."

"We both know you'll fall asleep as soon as I start talking."

He waves his pink handkerchief in the air and lets it float to the ground. I lean forward to pick it up, and he snatches it quickly.

"Remember that night? When I pricked your finger?" he asks.

"I remember. I still don't know why you did it."

"I gather samples. Of potential rebels. This way, we can always find you."

"As if I'm going anywhere," I respond.

"And by the way, that Cicero lies to you."

"What do you mean, Aurelio?"

"Rusty. Remember? Call me Rusty." He repositions himself to rest on his elbow. "Hey, so how do you think I lost this leg, *pendejo*."

"You've never told me."

"You never asked."

"I asked. You wouldn't talk about it. And, I didn't want to make you uncomfortable."

As soon as I say that I realize how stupid I sound.

"América is reckless. That's how."

"América?"

"That *pendejo* Cicero is right about one thing. América escaped."

"How do you know she escaped?"

Aurelio nods his head toward a brown White Guard, who nods back at him. I avoid his stare. The guard sneers and blows a kiss. I'm assuming for Aurelio.

"Friend of yours?" I ask.

"Maybe. Maybe spies are everywhere, Alex. Maybe you need to have a little faith."

"Faith? In what?"

Aurelio shakes his head, sighs out loud and rests his head on the rag pillow but not before he pulls out his copy of *Discipline and Punish*. It's a tattered paperback, earmarked for his choice paragraphs about torture. He places the beloved copy under the lump of rags and arranges his head comfortably.

"Well?" he asks. "Don't keep me waiting."

I pause to watch you with Tamaya and the Descendant women. Some are shifters but have reasoned themselves into this incarnation in these cages. You study a map with them, and I see you point to a spot, and they nod in unison. One of the women taps your shoulder and speaks to you, directing you to another spot on the map spread out on the cage floor. You memorize the critical places marked with bright cobalt markings. I watch your expression, focused and almost troubled. But it's not trouble I see. You're processing intently, so intently that your eyes moisten as if to emit tears. Tamaya places something in your hand, an opaque piece of glass. You are being told something that Tamaya keeps from me. Too often now she refuses to trust me and instead confides in her Descendant friends. She says she wants to protect me from worry, but I worry because you're too young to hold secrets of the future.

You return to my side, and I continue.

PART 4

"And children's voices peal over and under the air.
You've been there lost in the remembering."
—Mary Chapin Carpenter

"We are the fallen angels returned to teach
/the tenderness of hands, the tough choice/
of heart."
—Lorna Dee Cervantes

REBELLION

I awoke in my apartment with a throbbing headache. I rubbed a pea-sized bump above my right ear. Had some object hit me during the explosions? I remembered that I had explored the length of a ceiling with constellations and, out of the blue, there was the Impresario. And the Residents. And the surgery chamber. Blasts had ruptured doors from hinges and Descendant shifters had run from fires spewing fumes and red embers. I remembered the girl in the white lace dress. And then it struck me. Tanda. The Impresario. The bomb she slipped into his pants. He was dead. I breathed deeply and slowly to calm my heart hammering in my chest.

I got dressed and rushed to the café. Answers to my questions rolled on the television suspended from the ceiling. Old footage. América was right. Already Ascendant-surveyors publicized the dead Impresario's former deeds in their power play to discredit him. It was as if they had been waiting, prepared for their moment. The ASSES were ready to install their new puppet.

A huge screen streamed images of the Impresario reclining on a couch with four youngsters, all dressed scantily in lace underwear and lace bras that covered flat chests; they were that young. The Impresario draped his arms around two children and scoffed into the camera, proudly clinching his captives. Another elderly, slimy man entered the frame, leering and mocking the bulging eye of the lens that documented the vile treatment of their prisoners. He too wrapped an arm around a prepubescent girl whose face was blank. Probably drugged. With woozy, half-open eyelids and limp arms, the girls sat motionless. The men snorted and, despite the muted hum, the repulsive duo's guffaws sprang from the taped images.

The Impresario's infamous companion dipped his sharp jawline sideways, assuming defiance. I remembered his face spread on the front page of *The Hungry Hawk* just a week ago. Dressed in a dapper suit and tie, he smiled smugly. Above his photo the headlines read: "Impresario's Valued Statesman Murdered." Buried in the corner of the second page was his bashed-in face, unrecognizable. The official story targeted a gang of Descendant orphans who attempted to rob him, and when he resisted, they smashed his face with a cinder block. The facts were sketchy at best. A reporter on the scene had bribed a White Guard, who informed him that the dead man's wallet was filled with money, and his gold watch, worth half a million dollars, still bejeweled his wrist. It seems the "valued statesman" had attempted to blackmail the Impresario for starring in snuff films, murdering the girls he raped. Somewhere out there these films existed, but no one could find them after the murder of his accomplice with the bashed-in face. That this video was being broadcast now that the Impresario was dead meant the snuff films had surfaced from some power broker's vault.

Tamaya sat in a corner of the café with Lucy. As Tamaya lectured, Lucy frowned and spoke louder, spraying saliva onto Tamaya's cheeks. Her dark brown freckles reddened, while Tamaya seemed unmoved, calmly surveying the room. When she saw me, she left Lucy screaming after her.

"About time you got here," said Tamaya.

She joined me at my small, wobbly table. Why did I consistently find the most lopsided tables? Nervous, I bent down and jimmied a folded envelope from my pocket beneath one of the legs to secure it from wobbling.

"Where did you go, Tamaya?" I asked. "After the rescue? And after, well, you know." I nodded my head toward the screen, which was running the footage on a loop.

"Another mission."

"Those girls?"

"Yes. Those girls. And others. All safe now," she said.

"Why didn't you tell me?"

"You would have been useless if I'd told you."

"I was useless, anyway."

"Were you?"

I shrugged. "Aren't you afraid? They'll find us, won't they?"

"Maybe. Maybe not. Doesn't matter. We do what we must. *Y ya.*"

"But you've never murdered . . ." and I stopped. My heart pounded again.

"Come with me. I have something to show you," she said.

I gazed around the café and didn't notice any unusual customers. I relaxed.

"More mystery, Tamaya?"

"Not a mystery."

Merry-Go-Round

She glanced around the café and tipped her chin toward Lucy and Z. They dipped their heads, acknowledged her. I waved at the Rebels, but no one responded. I thought I'd made friends last evening. It was obvious that I remained on the periphery of whatever may have been happening in front of me, because something was happening.

Tamaya led the way out the back door, where the distinguishable, crammed junkyard expanded with each visit to the café. No one paid attention to the junk that was thrown onto more piles of junk. Rusted automobile skeletons, shattered computer monitors, broken vacuum cleaners, worn-out tires, ripped couches and chairs, and so many toaster ovens were piled high. I never had use for the kitchen gadget and never understood why the ovens were so popular, but here they were, stacked as proof of their usefulness until worn-out. The mountain of junk resembled a metallic monster, a colossal giant with long chords dangling at its sides like an octopi's arms.

"Why doesn't it tip over?" I mumbled out loud.

Tamaya stood beside me and looked up at the metal giant.

"It's leaning against that wall," she said.

"What wall? I don't see a wall."

She grabbed my hand and pulled me closer.

"It's invisible," she said.

174

"Oh."

I didn't see the wall, couldn't see it, and yet somehow, because Tamaya reassured me the wall existed, I believed her. Her reassurance eased me as I stood at the foot of this tall metallic pile of junk that could kill me if it toppled.

"We're here."

"Here? Here where?"

An antiquated carrousel with painted ponies, llamas, sheep, lions and one lone bear circled round with little girls riding the whimsical sculptures of animals. The slight girl who had been whimpering in the helicopter the night before held the leather reigns attached to the bear.

"Hidden in plain sight," I said.

Tamaya paused and counted, pointing to each girl and boy, finishing at the prime number of twenty-three.

"They'll need a safe place. That's where you come in," said Tamaya.

Just then from behind the carrousel, América emerged and interrupted, "It's okay. I'll help you."

"Where'd you come from?" I asked. I wasn't disappointed to see her.

"Somebody had to stay with them last night. I was here. With some of the other Rebels. Keeping watch. Keeping them safe. Anyway, I'm here to help you."

"Help me? With what?"

"Seems we have twenty-three charges to transport."

"But how? And to where?" I asked.

Tamaya and América looked at each other. I became uneasy.

"Until we find their families, we need a safe place. Somewhere no one will look for them," said Tamaya. "That's where you come in Alex."

"Me? I live in a small hovel of an apartment. With boxes of dusty, old books. Hardly a cozy sanctuary for these little folx."

"The Grand Library," said Tamaya.

"Are you crazy?"

"Probably."

"The Grand Library?" I addressed Tamaya. "Are you serious?"

"No one will search for them there. They'll be safe."

"But where? The Residents have access to every room."

"Not the archive room with Descendant records. You said so yourself."

I had to agree. No one had visited that part of the building for over a decade. Except me. And the area was spacious even with cluttered cartons and untouched documents crowding the corners. Worn out chairs and couches were dispersed among the filing cabinets, and there was a bathroom with running water and a shower. I kept an electric kettle and cups on a counter, and someone had left a cheap hot plate and a pan.

"I still don't agree that it's safe," I said.

"Safe enough . . . for now," said América.

"I have to run," said Tamaya.

"What? You're leaving now?" I asked.

"Alex, quit whining. América will help you. And look," she pointed to Lucy and Z, who pulled up in Fidel's heap of a car. "They'll drive the children over to the Library. And anyway, it's not that far. You can join them. Lead them to the archives."

"And you? Where are you going?" I was insistent because once again I refused to be tricked into Tamaya's dangerous operations.

"We can't waste time. The ASSES are busy bickering for power, and the White Guards are waiting for orders. It's a perfect time to raid more camps."

And with that, Tamaya disappeared. Again.

"Hiding them in the Library . . ." I said. "We're really doing this."

"We're really doing this," said América.

América whistled and waved to a group of young shifters, who lined up and squeezed into the jalopy. Z revved the engine, and I climbed in with the brood, while Lucy, who had been uncommonly quiet, stayed behind with América. I saw the girl, who was no longer whimpering, wave at me and smile. She seemed happy, gripping the reigns of a synthetic, blue bear.

THE ARCHIVES

Dropping them off and making them somewhat comfortable was easy enough. We drove up behind the building in one of the alleys that the Residents believed were too dangerous because they feared the young Rebels in cinder block homes that blocked the driveway. I'd avoided the back entrance myself but, today I had no choice. I jiggled the knob on the back door, hoping by some chance it was unlocked, but of course I was wrong. Z shoved me aside, wiggled the lock, poked a thin wire into a crack, and the door squeaked open slowly. The young shifters ran inside, skipping and hopping among cabinets and boxes and scattered furniture. That they were so joyful was infectious. Elated, I didn't care about the noise they were making. The thick walls were soundproof, and we were so far away from the center of the Library's main activities that, really, there was no need to tell them to be quiet. I didn't want to frighten them with precautions that were more than likely unnecessary.

"Do you suppose they're hungry?" I asked Z.

"Fidel's bringing a pot of stew over," Z said.

"Seems you all had this planned and figured out without me," I said.

Z, whose lanky body towered over mine, looked down at me. "We still need you, Alex."

"Z is right, we still need you." It was América.

She popped up out of nowhere with Lucy and the other kids. They had slipped inside through the unlocked door.

"How'd you get here so fast?" I asked.

Fidel followed behind, lugging a twenty-quart stock pot with enough stew to feed the rabble.

"Hibiscus stew," he said. "From my garden. They'll love it. Oh, and these."

He tossed a few dozen corn tortillas onto the counter that held the hot plate.

"Here Lucy, you can start heating these up," he said.

Lucy placed a pan on the hot plate that she had already plugged in.

"Let's go," said América, yanking on my arm. "They're set for the night."

"Yeah, don't worry about us. We got this," said Z.

I brushed off América and stepped away. "I know my way home," I insisted.

"I thought we could have an evening. Just you and me."

"You and me? Why?"

"Why not?"

I frowned and immediately regretted my hesitation.

"Damn, you're annoying Alex. Do you like living in limbo?"

"I don't live in limbo."

"Don't you?"

Lucy and Z were eavesdropping. They raised eyebrows at each other as if to declare some kind of agreement with América.

"I always thought you'd do more. Be more," said América.

The insistence in her voice didn't motivate me until she grabbed the flesh of my upper arm so tightly, I sprang back in pain. When I turned to scowl at her, she smiled good-heartedly and clasped my hand warmly.

"Time to go," she said. "It's getting late."

COLD NOODLES

We left the Library and crossed the vacant streets. The path to my apartment was lined with half-empty boutiques and vendors who had once thrived in Descendant neighborhoods. In the new Global Order, too many were too poor for modest luxuries like new clothes and shoes. Each week, another shop shut down because customers couldn't even purchase staples like beans or rice, much less a winter jacket. I admired Fidel because he kept a simple menu and weathered the rumors that the restaurant was a Rebel cell masquerading as a café, feeding all who might be starving with no means to pay.

We arrived at my apartments as the sun slid scarlet on the horizon behind decaying skyscrapers. América went to the living room window and surveyed the abandoned buildings. She watched the hawks flying above the wreckage. I paused beside her, and she clasped my hand and intertwined her fingers with mine. I feared the burn of her touch because I would be done for. Yet again. With a swift, tender push, América pressed me against the window, stepped behind me and brushed her lips against the nape of my neck. I trembled, and my legs quaked uneasily. I turned around to kiss her gently and instead mashed so vigorously against her mouth that she stumbled backwards, frowning and laughing reflexively. I regretted my awkwardness, yet she was undisturbed and led me to the lumpy couch, kissing my cheeks and eyelids until I was further undone. I traced the line of beauty marks below her eye inching to her mouth and I was grateful for what promised to be an uninterrupted night.

"Happy?" I asked.

"Overjoyed."

"Your enthusiasm is infectious."

She relaxed her head on my stomach, and I smoothed my hand over her crown's tight black curls and rubbed her temples. With my middle finger, I fondled her scalp and patted the mole I had once discovered. Each time we had met at the pond late at night to grope bodies, the fleshy bump lay bare beneath crimped locks as a reminder of identifiable traits that could not be erased.

"You know, you're the only one who has ever found the mole buried under my hair."

"It's not hard to find," I said.

"Apparently, hard enough."

"Does it bother you? That I search for it?"

"Not at all."

She paused and then announced, "It's your birthday next week."

"I know."

"Alejandra, Alejandra. Alex," she murmured.

After another protracted pause, she pinched her eyelids and looked up at me. "There's still time. You can go back."

"Go back?"

"To the Library," she said.

"To be Ben? Really?"

"Yeah, really."

"After all this? Return to those hypocrites?"

"If that's what you want."

I winced, unsure of what she meant.

"Hungry?" I asked.

"Only if you have chocolate cake."

I went into the kitchen and returned with cold noodles.

"Still a great chef, I see," she said.

"I didn't make this."

"They cook for you, don't they?"

"Who?"

"Your fleeting paramours."

"I don't know what you mean."

"All those women you cheat on . . . as Ben."

I shoved a forkful of noodles in her mouth, and she chewed heartily.

"Jealous?" I asked.

"My noodles are better."

She grabbed my fork and shoveled noodles in my mouth. "Come on. Let's get some sleep. Tomorrow's a busy day."

"Oh? What's on the agenda?"

"The usual. Revolution. And your birthday party."

"I don't want a birthday party."

"Sure, you do. And anyway, it's already planned. You'll love it."

"I guess I have no choice."

"Alejandra. There's always a choice."

Before we fell asleep, I wrapped my legs around hers. I'd convinced my body's memory that I had no past with América. Or Marco. But here she was. Here they were. Imprinted. Indelible. Dammit. Like a gut punch each time.

The sun had barely flickered through the window when her phone buzzed. América answered, and I could hear Lucy's panicked voice shrieking while América tried to quiet her down, telling Lucy to speak slowly. Her brows wrinkled and she puckered her lips as she rose from the bed and pulled a white shirt out of my closet. She quickly buttoned and tucked it into her jeans. With the phone locked between her shoulder and ear, she mouthed to me, "Coffee, please."

I tugged on khaki pants and a black T-shirt I found buried in a drawer full of young Ben's boyish wardrobe. The T-shirt fit snugly across my breasts. The lax cotton soothed my skin, which had become a darker hue each time I shifted and resolved to be Alejandra. In the kitchen, I hovered over a pot of espresso while waiting for América to emerge with news I wasn't prepared to hear. She dropped onto a spindly chair at the kitchen table, and I placed a demitasse of black espresso in front of her. She swallowed it down and held up the demitasse signaling for a refill.

"Are you going to tell me?"

"You don't want to know."

"I don't?"

"The café is gone. Blown up. The White Guard bombed it last night. Retaliation. For the Impresario. Some of the guards remain loyal to that asshole."

I couldn't move. "And Fidel?"

"No one has seen him. He may have been inside when it happened."

"Tamaya?"

"Not seen either."

"How many?"

"We can't be sure. Kindred shifters stayed late at the café celebrating after the rescue. Fidel brought out his old, hoarded tequila, and they were dancing and shifting. Lots of shifting and dancing. We knew we had an intruder, a plant, a spy for the White Guard, but I never thought they were capable of this. Lucy was suspicious. She's always suspicious, but I told her not to worry. She was right. Of course, she was right."

"One of Lucy's friends?" I asked. "Or Tamaya?" As soon as I spoke, I regretted what I'd allowed myself to consider.

"Oh, right. Tamaya is the spy. Seriously, Alejandra? Feeling guilty?"

I averted her glare and opened a kitchen cabinet, ferreting for a cup. I pushed aside dishes until one fell to the floor and shattered into two, imperfect flawless halves. I stooped to pick up the white, unadorned pieces and held the sides together at the broken edge.

"Just glue it. Or throw it away," she said.

I returned the shattered plate to the cabinet and closed the door.

"She doesn't care, you know," said América. "Quit feeling so guilty."

América sipped her second cup of espresso. She stared at a spot on the table, maybe to study something that could give her an answer, a plan. Or maybe she wanted to forget for that one minute. I put my hand on her shoulder, and she grabbed my fingers, wove them between hers and kissed my fingertips. My flesh tingled. There it was again. Her touch. Dammit.

"We need to go see," I said.

"Charred bodies?"

"We don't know that."

My desperation couldn't prod her. Instead, she poked at a greasy spot on the kitchen table and rubbed the grease with her palm.

"Don't you clean?" she asked.

She carried on, chafing the spot.

"It's a stain," I said. "A permanent stain. Nothing gets it out."

She nodded. When she stood up, I anticipated her breath on my face. Without purpose, she snatched my brown, leather wallet from my front pocket and shoved it into my back pocket, pulled it back out and shoved it deeper into the front pocket again.

"Okay. Let's go. We have to see," she said.

ASHES

The scene wasn't what we foresaw. We considered that the building would have been gutted, but in the spot where the café had been, had always been, we saw ashes piled high. There were no skeletons or vestiges of anything. No charred bodies, no teeth, no remnants, nothing. All had vanished. Extinct. Tamaya stood in the rubble, hands hoisted on her hips. As we drew near, we saw her head quiver and tears, mottled with gray ash, streaming down her cheeks.

"Took you long enough," she said, eyeballing me, and spat on the cinders at my feet.

"Fidel?" I asked.

"Look around, Alex. You're probably standing on him."

I lifted my feet from the ashes and dabbed tears swelling up in me. I was so relieved to see her.

"How did you survive?" I had to ask.

Tamaya pivoted to face me.

"Well?" I asked.

"I wasn't here," she answered.

When she spun around, embers from the heap scattered and floated into the air. Ashen clouds staged an otherworldly image of cinders drifting and hovering above her body, a scrim of light poked through the particles.

"Where's Lucy?" asked América.

"I don't know. Why?"

"When she called me, she said something . . . about the Grand Library."

"What about it?" asked Tamaya.

"I thought she was with the kids. At the Library," I said.

"They aren't *just* kids." It was Z who appeared from some-where—I wasn't sure from where, with the mess of fragments and mounds of ashes.

"They aren't just kids," Z said. "They're shifters. Kindred shifters. Soul folx. Why is it so hard?"

Z flicked through the residue and brushed a boot across the powder, sculpting wide circles.

"And to answer your question, of course, she wasn't here. That was the plan."

"What plan?" I asked.

"We aren't ready," said Tamaya. "Dammit, Lucy."

FIDEL

We circled around to a recognizable path. When we arrived at the crossroads to the Grand Library, the streets were quiet, deserted. A sudden pang in my chest overwhelmed me. We strode closer and stopped in a grassy park. Clouds loomed, casting furtive figures on the grass.

Standing firm on a knoll was Fidel, and I waved eagerly while running to him.

He shouted words I couldn't recognize.

"Wait," said América. "He's warning us."

"Warning us? What?"

"He's pointing at us. Get down," said América.

"Why? What . . . ."

Fidel shouted, and when he realized we couldn't hear him, he waved but not to greet us. He signaled a warning, gesturing what Rebels had agreed upon. With his right palm open, fingers outstretched, he tapped his left fist twice. Danger. America and Tamaya shoved me down hard, and we ducked from gunfire. But the bullets weren't for us. Slugs mauled Fidel as if he was a punching bag. No, that's wrong. As if he was a paper silhouette for target practice. Riddled with jagged holes.

América held me close and thrust my face into the crook of her arm. When I peeked up, I fixed on the constellation of moles on her right cheek. Five black beauty marks I'd memorized not only for their beauty but also for the way they mapped something else, a better place maybe. Tamaya crawled to Z, who was hunched near other young Rebels, their faces so close that tears cascading from their cheeks looked like a single stream.

We were in too much shock to move after sequences of gunfire had done their duty on Fidel and nothing was left except a red corpse oozing blood from every place. We were in too much shock to see what came next. An explosion rocked the boulevard, and our bodies flew suspended in the air, landing on gravel and concrete. And there she was: Lucy. She looked in our direction and waved, then fled into the inferno streaming from the foyer of the Grand Library. I never saw her again.

PART 5

"No fences or walls would stop them;
guns and bombs would not stop them.
They had no fear of death;
they were comfortable with their ancestors' spirits.
They would come by the millions."
—Leslie Marmon Silko

PORTALS AND SPIRITS

With guns aimed at our backs, we were herded into green
military trucks already crowded with other Descendants, who
squeezed together not only for lack of space but also in hopes
of protecting each other. We were no different. I wedged between América and Tamaya. When we arrived at some unknown
place of detention, we were separated, and I didn't see either of
them again until a few days later, but it was only Tamaya who
was hurled into our cage. She had bribed a White Guard, who
was actually her cousin, to allow her to join me. She persuaded
him that we were married, which in fact, was not the case. Neither of us condoned marriage, but Tamaya was well aware of
the sentimentalities that could affect some of the Guards, especially if they were from one's own family. Her cousin reckoned
that Tamaya had been led down the wrong road of rebellion and
was justifiably imprisoned. He was one of those Descendants
who denied his origins, ashamed of his ancestors and unwilling
to confess his own propensity to shift. The fact that many could
shift. And many feared it,

❧❧❧

Tears run down my cheeks.

"You blame Fidel," you say. "He was the spy. All along. Wasn't he?"

"I don't blame him," I say.

"You fucking blame him and you know it." It was Rusty. He sat up and pulled his leg out straight. "Sometimes, I blame him and I loved him. Anyway, it was my fault. He did it for me. And our family. He did it for everyone. How do you think he had enough money to feed anybody who came into the café? Huh? He did it for us. For the cause. For the rebellion. We're all to blame. You know why they shot him like that? To show us. That they can do what the fuck they want. Yeah sure, Fidel was a spy but he never turned his back on us. In the end, he warned you. You know he did."

I was too exhausted to argue or comment on everything Rusty had just said. I knew he was right about Fidel.

"You need to rest, Papi," you say.

"I'm too tired to rest, *m'ija*."

"Close your eyes," you tell me.

I do. I close my eyes and soar into a vast blue sky with clouds that disperse, vaporizing into fog, and I dream again finding solace in the dream. It is as if the fog takes me into an unknown consciousness that provides another way of being, another dimension. You've taught me about the fifth and seventh dimensions, assuring me we will time travel into the past and the future, but I'm as ever doubtful of the theories you and your mother concoct.

"It's not a concoction, Papi. You'll see," you say to me.

More than once you have assured me that time is false. Not a thing at all but something we fall back on as reassurance.

"Reassurance of what, *m'ija*?" I ask.

"Simple, Papi. That we'll see each other again."

I'm only assured that I won't see you again.

IT'S TIME

I'm in a deep sleep when someone shakes my leg, rousing me to wake up. It's Tamaya.

"Alejandra. It's time."

"It's too soon."

"It's time," she repeats.

"I can't. Not without her."

Only Tamaya knows who I mean.

Reluctantly, I shake myself awake and join Tamaya and her folx of shifter Descendants. Many have chosen to be female, others still shift when desiring to do so. I already know they've located the portal and have mapped our journey. I can't help but cry. Tamaya wipes tears from my face.

"She's not here, Alex. You know that. Yareli's gone. She escaped. We arranged it. You know that. It was time."

I'm sobbing. Tamaya grabs my arm and tugs me behind her. I can't tell her I'm also crying for América. I don't want to tell her, or anyone, that I dream about América and haven't stopped loving her. That I guard her secret because dreams of her comfort me through all this chaos. Tamaya wouldn't care. Not really. She understands that love takes many forms and, while we both love América, I'm the one who writes to her in my head. Over and over, I miss her like a wheel rounding corners, infinite circles, round and round, a carrousel going nowhere. Trapped in the missing of her. All wound up and mottled with you, Yareli. So confusing to lose so many at once and speculate you'll never see them again and, if you do, it won't matter because they'll be someone else and you too will be something else, and all you shared will have dissipated like fog. What is it about revolution so many fear? The changes? The transformations looming over us for centuries and, yet nothing. Few are willing to leap, to move, to go to that place of newness. Are we on the brink again? You seem to have faith. I often doubt that another way of being is on the horizon, but you, you remain hopeful.

"I am hopeful, Papi," you respond.

At least I think I hear you respond, but you're nowhere near. The lights fade into darkness, and I only hear breathing. Easy, temperate breaths lull the atmosphere in the cages. Tamaya takes my hand. We follow her friends, all the Descendant women who have been calculating the opening of a window, a door, a portal. Unexpectedly, a young brown White Guard leads us through a tunnel, and I'm immediately suspicious.

"Tamaya, this isn't right," I say to her.

"Yes, it is. Have a little faith, Alejandra."

"No, it can't be right."

I scan the darkness and focus enough to see we're in single file, hundreds of us, maybe more, following the brown young man.

I hear murmurs in the tunnel, but the voices rise from elsewhere, not from any of us marching single file into an infinite space. The portal is open and the ancestors are waiting.

"... a real fucking revolution is, at its core, spiritual."
—Ali, "Euphoria," December 4, 2020

"So what are you?" They asked, being very perplexed.
Buddha simply replied: "I am awake."
—Buddhist teaching

July 29, 2069

Yareli sits cross-legged on a cushion inside a room with glass panels stretching from an oak floor, high above to a thin veil of lingering fog. Outside the glass, a garden teems with rose bushes, pink peonies, barrel cacti, hibiscus, vegetables and herbs. Golden zucchini flowers saturate the patch, cherry tomatoes are ripe and the smell of basil permeates the warm breeze. Vines of mint wrap around a four-foot wooden fence. She's not alone. Beside her are dozens of young shifters, teens and into their twenties and thirties, like Yareli. A chime is heard, and they all rise and roam the room, stepping over flat, multicolored cushions, open-armed and embracing. These Descendant ceremonies soothe and uplift them, preparing them for other dimensions, for transcendence, for more that is to come. Yareli wears ripped jeans and a white T-shirt with the name and photograph of some steam-punk-goth-R&B band.

She opens glass double doors covered with razor etchings of emoji caricatures resembling bunnies, wolves, snakes, and hawks. Carved throughout the glass is the symbol "W5" that young Rebels still advocated and still believed—"we will win the Woke Wars." Past the doors, a shelf with shoes and boots are piled. Yareli steps inside olive green combat boots and laces them securely.

"Yareli," María calls and gestures at her to follow.

María wears her signature white lace dress like the one she wore the night she was rescued, and when she smiles, two discernable wrinkles adorn the corners of her mouth. She takes Yareli's hand and leads her through hallways and into the Grand Library's principal room. It's the only room that survived the many insurrections that brought the young Descendant shifters here. Filled with bookshelves, rectangular tables and desks, it's the space Yareli treasures. They pause in front of a desk once reserved for male scholars—the Residents. This one holds value for Yareli, but not for its vintage design. The relic had been where Benito Espinoza wrote books. The desk is her chosen station. The tables and desks are crowded with Descendant shifters—brown, black and white. Some play computer games while wearing goggles that transport them into some virtual reality and others design cities and streets with railways and bicycle paths. There are those who ferret through dusty boxes crammed with photographs and journals. Daily, Yareli scours looking for something she'll recognize.

"This was dropped off . . . this morning," says María.

"Who dropped . . . ?"

"No one knows. It was placed in the foyer with this note."

Yareli takes the piece of paper and checks her name scribbled in red ink. A dark mahogany box the size of a bulky, picture book rests on the desk. It has a lock and no key.

"I know," says María. "I can solve that puzzle."

She extracts from her head a hairpin, jiggles the lock and opens it effortlessly.

Yareli lifts a compact blue notebook with brown lines and nearly two-hundred pages. A sepia photograph falls from inside. She picks it up, holds it out and scrutinizes the three figures pictured. Two women in camouflage garb brandish swords across their chests. Razor-sharp tips point diagonally to the sky. Between them, stands her papi with short, wavy, dark hair, dressed in khaki pants, pink dress shirt and a cashmere, beige jacket with felt elbow patches. Yareli flips the snapshot and reads the names: "Tamaya, Alejandra, América." In the photograph, her parents are smiling. The date is April 11th. A spring day. No year. They stand like victorious heroes beaming with promise, and while cautious, willing to embrace their victory. At the bottom left corner, she spots a message. *"Yareli, pass on our stories. And when you're ready, come find me. You'll know where to look. Love, América."* Yareli caresses the blue notebook, opens to the first page, and reads: "Let me tell you how my body shifted. Just shifted."